MARY, WILL I DIE?

MARY, WILL I DIE ?

SHAWN SARLES

SCHOLASTIC PRESS
NEW YORK

3948678

Library of Congress Cataloging-in-Publication Data available

ISBN 978-1-338-67927-4

1 2021

Printed in the U.S.A.   23

First edition, September 2021

Book design by Yaffa Jaskoll

To my parents, Linda and Richard,
who were my first and biggest fans

PROLOGUE
ELENA

She knew she should have been scared. She should have been curled up in a ball, her hands thrown over her head for protection, cowering in a basement, sheltering in place. That was where everyone else would be right now. But for what?

How many times had the sky turned black and the winds blown hard? How often had the clouds steepled into angry, furrowed masses threatening to unleash Armageddon? And yet, the sun always came out fifteen minutes later. The danger never materialized. Never did any damage.

A siren started wailing outside. It cut through the howling wind that rattled every window in the house.

"We should go back downstairs," a voice whimpered from behind Elena.

"Don't be such a baby," Elena snapped at Grace, her best friend, though sometimes she wondered how much longer she'd be able to put up with the girl. "Nothing's going to happen."

"I don't know," another girl spoke up. "It sounds pretty bad out there."

"I think Steph's right," a boy added, his glasses sliding down his nose so that he had to keep pushing them back up over and over again.

"Fine. Go back to your boring lives."

Elena was so over them. All three of them.

Grace. Steph. And Calvin.

Her carpool buddies, though she was only actually friends with Grace. They were all in the same fourth-grade class, and her mom had picked them up early today because of the storm warning.

"But if you want to see something cool and prove that you're not a scaredy-cat, then follow me."

At first no one responded to Elena's challenge, but then Grace took the bait, like Elena knew she would.

"Cool like what?" she asked, her voice a nervous whisper.

"You're about to find out."

Elena's mouth split into a wicked grin and she started down the hallway, glancing over her shoulder, satisfied when Grace's surrender dominoed into Steph's and Calvin's. All three were following her now, marching up to the closed door in single file.

"What's in there?" Grace squeaked.

"A ghost."

Elena delighted in the shiver that shook Grace, the shocked O rounding the girl's lips. Then, before anyone could recover, she reached up and twisted the handle, swinging the door open and revealing the black cavern of a room. She slipped inside and waited for them to join her.

Lightning flickered beyond the curtained windows, the flash spotlighting the room in black and white. It pulsed again, and this time someone yelped as a shrouded figure lunged out of the shadows. Grace threw herself into Elena as she dove for the door. Before she could bolt, though, Elena reached over and pulled the string on an old lamp. Its golden glow filled the room and revealed the ghostly figure for what it was—a piece of furniture, a sheet thrown over it to keep off the dust.

"It's only a bedroom," Steph commented, and a frown wrinkled her forehead.

"It's not," Elena said.

The wind howled against the windows as Elena paused, relishing what would come next.

"It's my grandmother's room. At least—it *was*."

An eerie calm settled around them, like they'd suddenly been sucked into the eye of a tornado. Elena could almost feel her ears pop as the air pressure shifted and grew brittle.

"When did she die?" Calvin asked, his voice hushed.

"A few months ago." Elena said.

"I'm sorry," Steph mumbled.

"Don't be," Elena replied before she could check herself.

Before she realized how heartless it sounded. "I mean, she was pretty old and out of it at the end."

That was true, at least. In those last few weeks of her life, Elena's grandmother had spiraled into a ghoul. Her fingers had narrowed into hooked talons. Her hair stuck straight out from her head in patchy white wisps. Nonsense had rattled from her mouth night and day, a feverish rant, her native German only broken up here and there by a random English word. But even those Elena could hardly understand.

Her mom had tried to explain it to her. Something called dementia. It stole her grandmother's memories. Twisted them. Made her see things that weren't there. Made her rant at the very air in front of her face. Invisible enemies hiding in the shadows.

"And all this . . . is hers?" Grace asked, her question quiet. Reverent. Elena had talked about the woman with Grace, but they'd never actually met. And Elena hadn't told her when her grandmother had passed. She hadn't even invited her to the funeral.

"It was," Elena replied. Her grandmother had moved in near the end, bringing with her a few of her most prized possessions. Which reminded Elena . . .

Before anyone could say another word, she flounced across the room and grabbed the edge of the hanging sheet, tugging on the fabric and letting it unfurl. The shroud flowed to the floor and pooled around the wooden legs of the imposing relic, revealing the bogeyman for what it was—a mirror.

"That looks really old," Calvin marveled, the first to find his voice.

"And expensive," Steph piped up, moving in to get a closer look. "Are those real?"

Tentatively, the girl reached forward but stopped, her finger hovering less than an inch above one of the pearl-like orbs inset all the way around the mirror's flawless glass.

"I don't know," Elena replied. "It's been in my grand-mother's family for generations or something."

"Are these hers, too?" Grace asked, her pipsqueak voice interrupting Elena, who spun around and saw the girl fingering the knickknacks on top of the dresser. The antique silver rings and necklaces that could use polishing. A photo album and some old books.

"Yeah. It was all hers."

"Cool." The word was barely audible as Grace continued to sift through it all. Elena tapped her foot in the middle of the room, crossing her arms as she turned and saw Calvin still mesmerized by the mirror, his nose an inch from the glass.

This wasn't much fun anymore. Not for her. They were supposed to be shocked and scared. They might as well have stayed downstairs.

But then, as Elena was about to suggest that they wrap things up, she caught a movement in the mirror. Her own annoyed face reflected behind Calvin's. But there was a twinkle in her eye. A smirk on her lips. And suddenly, an idea struck her.

"Let's play a game," Elena said, her voice coaxing everyone to listen. "It's called Bloody Mary."

The light in the room dimmed and the wind picked up outside, howling against the side of the house, reminding everyone that there was a storm brewing. Elena pushed Calvin aside and stepped in front of the mirror.

"It's simple, as long as you don't scare easy."

And Elena went on to explain the rules.

"All you have to do is stare into the mirror. Right at your reflection. And then you say *Bloody Mary* thirteen times."

She didn't know where this had come from. It was almost like a spirit was standing right behind her, whispering the directions into her ear for her to repeat. But it sounded good. It sounded scary.

"What happens then?" Steph asked, clearly unimpressed by the game.

"Well, you wait." Elena strung it out to buy some time, examining her own reflection as if her mirror version might have the answer. "And then Bloody Mary shows you your soulmate's face."

Elena liked that. Especially since she'd come up with it on the spot. But it needed more. Something extra. Something twisted.

"Or," Elena began, "you'll see Bloody Mary's horrible face. A sign that you're going to die young. Maybe even tonight."

And a clap of thunder crashed overhead, adding that perfect exclamation point to her words.

"Here, I'll go first."

Before anyone could protest or call her silly, Elena stepped right up to the mirror, looked her reflection dead in the eye, and started speaking.

"Bloody Mary. Bloody Mary. Bloody Mary."

The name rolled off her tongue like some kind of incantation. And everyone in the room was under its spell, sucking in their breaths as they waited to see what would happen. Even the storm outside seemed to be listening.

"Bloody Mary."

As she spoke the name for the thirteenth time, Elena rose up on her tiptoes, leaning closer to the mirror so that her nose almost grazed the glass. Her gaze pierced through her reflection, looking for something. Anything. Even she had gotten swept up in her game. Even she believed that Bloody Mary might reveal something to her.

With a blinding flash and a violent crack, the storm broke back into the room. Elena jumped and Grace let out a whimper. Then something above them snapped and the room was suddenly plunged into complete darkness.

Elena could hear the others panicking around her—Grace's soft keening, Steph's sharp gasp, Calvin's pitchy yelp—but none of that mattered.

Because she'd seen something. She swore it. There, in that

split second before the lights had gone out, there'd been a face. A boy from her class. One she had a crush on. Henry. Her soulmate.

"Did you see that?" Elena spun around, fishing her phone out of her pocket so that she could use the flashlight app. "There was a face in the mirror."

But no one else seemed to believe her.

"You must have missed it when the lights went out." Elena sounded disappointed. But she wasn't defeated. "Here. One of you go."

"I think we should head downstairs," Steph replied. "Your mom will probably be looking for us. And I don't want to get in trouble."

Elena frowned. But then Grace stepped up.

"I'll go."

Her hand dipped nervously into one of the pockets of her skirt, but she took her place in front of the mirror. She peered into it, using Elena's phone to see, and spoke the name just like the other girl had, pausing after the thirteenth time and holding her breath.

"Did you see anything?" Elena asked after only a couple of seconds. Grace's cheeks had turned bright red. But she only shook her head as she shuffled back, doing her best not to make eye contact with anyone.

"Calvin, give it a try."

And Elena pushed the boy in front of her, holding the light

up again as she coaxed him into repeating the name. As it crossed Calvin's lips for the last time, he suddenly froze, the color draining completely from his face.

"Who'd you see?" Elena asked. Because once again she hadn't spotted anything in the mirror.

"No one," Calvin stuttered. "There wasn't anything there."

"Can we go now?" Steph asked from the door. She was pulling at her curly hair.

"Fine," Elena relented. "But first you have to take your turn. Don't you want to see who your true love is?"

Steph rolled her eyes, but Elena stood firm. She wasn't going to move until they'd all gone. This time she wasn't even going to blink. She would make sure she didn't miss whoever's face appeared.

Steph dragged her feet across the room and gave Elena another annoyed look before facing the mirror and half-heartedly rattling off the thirteen *Bloody Marys*.

But then, something in her eyes changed. Her shoulders tensed, and the annoyed scowl slid from her face, shock replacing it. And maybe fear. However, before Elena could ask Steph what she'd seen, her mother's voice wailed through the house, vaulting up the stairs, hunting them down.

The kids exchanged a quick glance and bolted out of the room. Elena was last, and as she paused to shut the door, she glanced one last time at the mirror, feeling it calling to her. She squinted, and she thought she saw something glimmer in the glass. A shadow dancing in the reflection, swaying gently back and forth. She could have sworn she heard a low purr. A triumphant giggle. But then her mother shouted again and Elena forgot the vision. She slammed the door and raced down the stairs. When she caught up to everyone else, her mother wore a panicked look. But she couldn't seem to find the words to explain her dismay.

"Mom, what's wrong?" Elena asked, her heart suddenly racing, thumping in her ears. "Is it Dad? Is he okay?"

"He's fine."

Elena relaxed. For a second.

"But Grace—" Elena's mom turned to the girl, crouching in front of her. "Now, listen, sweetie, everything's going to be okay. But your mom—she's been in a car accident. She got hurt pretty bad."

Grace didn't move, her round eyes suddenly dead. Her hands fell to her sides, slapping against her legs. Steph's mouth dropped open and Calvin collapsed in on himself, biting his lip as he stared at the ground, clearly shaken.

"But they got her to the hospital," Elena's mom rushed to reassure the girl. "And your dad's on his way to pick you up now. She's going to be okay. You'll see. You just have to have faith."

Faith won't help her now.

Elena startled as the thought popped into her head. She looked over her shoulder as if she'd see someone whispering into her ear. But there was no one there.

As Grace started to weep softly and the winds continued to blow outside, Elena couldn't help thinking back to that face she'd seen in the mirror.

To Henry.

And she couldn't help wondering if he really was her soulmate.

CHAPTER 1
GRACE

The doors creaked shut behind her, groaning like the Cryptkeeper's coffin as Grace stepped off the school bus. She watched the other kids scatter in front of her, running to meet their friends, whooping and hollering like they hadn't seen one another the day before. Like they hadn't group-chatted all night long. Grace's hand fluttered to the necklace hanging around her neck, but she fought off the urge, pulling her backpack tight against her shoulders instead.

Freshman year of high school was supposed to be hard. She knew that. Everything was different. Her classmates and teachers. The building. All the electives and extracurriculars. There was a whole new set of rules for getting by. For just surviving. But she'd never imagined it would be this lonely.

Grace buried her chin in her chest and started walking, skirting between groups, trying her best to stay invisible but at the same time—oddly—wanting to be seen. She made it to the entrance but stopped short as her reflection caught her off guard. There, in the depths of the glass doors, her big eyes stared back at her, a message primed on the tip of her mirror tongue.

You'll never be pretty enough.

And she wouldn't. Not with her round face. Not with the limp brown bangs hanging across her forehead. Not with her pudgy cheeks and shapeless body. She took a step back so she could see it all, running her palms over her rumpled Mistress of the Dark T-shirt, smoothing out Elvira's bouffanted head and bright red lipstick. But not even the Mistress could take away the sting, the ugly feeling of being ugly.

This time Grace couldn't fight it. Her hand flew to her neck and snagged on the thin silver chain. She fished out the locket and stared at it, the charm shining in the morning light. She rubbed her fingers against the smooth metal and then opened it.

A woman looked back at her from the miniature black-and-white photograph, sitting with her head tilted toward the camera, dark hair swooping into a neat updo, skin flawless, her cheeks shadowed by good bone structure.

This was beauty. And it was copied there in the tiny mirror opposite the photo. If Grace squinted, she could almost imagine it was her own reflection. Her own features, passed down from generation to generation.

But who was she kidding? She'd never look like that. Never be so thin and elegant. Never be pretty.

Grace snapped the locket shut and tucked it back underneath her shirt. Then she dipped her head down, making sure to avoid her reflection this time as she pulled open the school door and walked inside.

The halls bustled around her, charged with their usual rhythm and flow, completely oblivious to her. But there was something different in the air this morning. A crispness that Grace couldn't pinpoint. Then she spotted the flyers tacked up everywhere, the orange papers smoldering along the walls. And she remembered why she had broken out her Elvira T-shirt. It was October first.

She plucked a flyer off the wall and made her way to her locker, walking absently as she read through the info.

The Harvest Halloween Carnival.

The high school sponsored the festival every fall. Students put together booths to raise money for their athletic teams and after-school clubs and Winter Formal. It was open to the whole town, so Grace had gone many times with her dad, every year since her mother—

Her breath caught in her throat and a pain lanced into her chest. She pressed the locket underneath her shirt, and its presence grounded her. Kept those lonely thoughts away. For now.

She looked back at the flyer and memorized the dates. The carnival always took place the week before Halloween. And while she'd been several times, she'd never gotten to go on open-ing night, when the carnival was reserved for the high school students only, letting them kick things off with a costumed blowout, minimal adult supervision. This was the first year she'd get to go, and she couldn't wait.

Carefully, Grace folded the flyer and bent over. She slung her backpack off her shoulders and slid the piece of paper into one of its pockets. She'd have to figure out a costume. And it'd have to be something good. Something that would make people notice her.

Halloween—monsters and ghosts and spooky stuff—it was kind of Grace's thing. In the dark, hidden under a layer of makeup and an over-the-top wig, costume jewelry swinging from her neck and studding her fingers, she could escape. She could be anyone and anything.

Zipping her backpack, Grace started to rise but froze half-way. A breath caught in her throat, but this time it was accompanied by a flutter in her stomach instead of a stabbing pain. Up ahead on the stairwell landing, a boy sat all by himself.

An outcast like her. A cute one. Calvin Lee. She'd had a crush on him ever since they'd shared a carpool in elementary school. But he hardly noticed her existence anymore. Or any-one's, really. He always had his nose stuck in his notebook, scribbling away, lost in his own world.

Not that Grace had noticed. It wasn't like she'd been watching him for years. Waiting for him to say hello. To make a move. To fall in love with her.

She shook her head, but kept watching Calvin.

She knew that it was silly and probably all in her head, but she remembered that day. The day of the accident. The day her mother—

The day they'd taken turns standing in front of Elena's grandmother's mirror. Grace had spoken that name—Bloody Mary—into the mirror and she'd felt a chill run up her spine. She'd seen someone hidden there in the depths of her reflection. Recognized Calvin's face. Her soulmate.

Which meant she just had to wait. If she'd seen him, then he must have seen her. They must be destined for each other.

"Out of the way," a voice crackled, ripping Grace out of her fantasy. She stumbled forward and barely managed to spring to her feet without face-planting. Clutching her backpack, she turned around and met the glossy lips and perfect blonde hair of her harasser. Her former best friend.

"I said move." Elena waved her sparkly fingernails in front of Grace's face, snapping impatiently. "You're blocking my locker."

The two girls flanking Elena had a good giggle as Grace shuffled out of the way, her shoulders hunched while her ears burned bright.

"What are you even wearing?"

Grace pulled her backpack to her chest to block Elvira's witchy face.

"What a freak," Elena muttered as she threw her bag into her locker and checked her reflection in the mirror she had hanging there. Grace watched as Elena puckered her lips and fluffed her hair. As Elena pulled out a tube of lip gloss and reapplied, in the background of the mirror, Grace caught a glimpse of her own flat brown hair.

She's right. You are a freak.

Grace tried to shake the words out of her head. There was a reason she avoided mirrors. She hated what she saw in her reflection. Hated the mean things she couldn't keep herself from thinking. She didn't need someone like Elena telling her she was ugly and a freak. She had the insults covered on her own.

"Henry," Elena gasped, and Grace blinked away from the mirror. She'd been so lost in thought that she hadn't noticed the boy sneaking up behind Elena. He wrapped his arms around her waist and lifted her into the air. Elena wiggled out of the boy's grip and turned to face him. She planted a kiss on his cheek and marked him as hers, leaving a glistening impression with her wet lip gloss.

Grace watched the couple for a second, and then backed away. If only she could be pretty like Elena. Pretty and popular. Then she wouldn't be so lonely. And Calvin might notice her. Might even ask her out.

Her eyes fluttered up to the stairwell landing, but Calvin

wasn't there. He couldn't have gone far. But as Grace thought about hunting him down, the first bell rang.

As she was scrambling up the stairs, though, a piece of paper caught her eye, lying flat on the floor right where Calvin had been sitting. She bent down to pick it up, and when she turned it over, a strange feeling hiccuped in her chest. A jolt of something sweet.

There on the paper was a sketch of what looked like some sort of demon. Almost an Elvira look-alike, with its tight dress and dark hair. Its lips were outlined in bright red. A drip of blood ran down its chin. Its eyes were possessed, ghastly.

Grace glanced over her shoulders to make sure no one else had seen. Then she whipped a notebook out of her backpack and carefully pressed the sketch in between the pages, keeping it safe and crisp. She felt light-headed and hopeful as her mind raced and her stomach flipped. Because maybe she and Calvin had something in common after all. Maybe they really were soulmates.

CHAPTER 2
CALVIN

The clamor in the cafeteria was overwhelming as Calvin got in line to get his food. He liked the noise, though. Craved it, even. He opened his ears and let the chaos fill him up.

Trays clattered as they were set down on tables. Forks and spoons tapped out their own percussion line. Mouths chewed, teeth chomped and tore between stories told, jokes were made, and dates were planned out. It was all music to Calvin's ears, because it distracted him. It prevented other things from rushing in.

As he made it to the end of the lunch line, Calvin paid and spun around to hunt for a seat. He didn't eat in the cafeteria often, so he didn't have a usual table. He didn't really have friends to pal around with either. It was better that way. It kept him from losing his mind. Well, from losing it any more than he already had.

Calvin spotted an open chair in the corner of the room. A seat at a half-empty table that faced the wall. Ideal real estate. However, as Calvin set off to claim it, a hissing jerked his attention away and he couldn't help turning to look.

The kitchen doors had swung open and a lunch lady had emerged, a fresh vat of bubbling sloppy joe mix in her arms. She breezed past Calvin without incident, but in that brief window before the doors could swing shut, Calvin had seen too much.

Knives gleamed sharply on countertops. An unattended pot had started to boil over on the stove. A package of meat had been left out, bacteria colonies most likely claiming territory on its red rawness.

Calvin blinked away, but having seen danger, his mind couldn't ignore it anymore. On the other side of the cafeteria, a table broke out in a chorus of "Happy Birthday" as a girl lit a couple of candles and stuck them in a cupcake. An apple fell off another table, rolling across the floor, getting kicked like a soccer ball, passed forward, just waiting for someone to miss, to step on it and be sent flying into the open jaws of the scorching-hot dishwasher.

Calvin blinked again, but he could only see hazard. He could only imagine worst-case scenarios. Accidents. Broken bones. Third-degree burns. Cuts that would bleed out and require fifteen stitches to seal back.

The images flooded his brain. They set his heart racing. He gritted his teeth and tried to push them back, but that didn't work. It never did. He took one last longing look at that empty chair in the corner of the room—the one where he would have been able to stare at the wall and eat his lunch in peace. Then he dropped his tray on a nearby table and booked it out of there, staring down at the floor so that he wouldn't pick up anything else.

As Calvin set off down the empty halls, his feet took him where he needed to go. They carried him past the gym and down the science wing. They took him into the library and through the stacks to the back, depositing him in the reference section at a scrawled-on desk.

Sitting, Calvin let his fingers wander across the old wood, feeling the grooves and gouges that generations of students had left behind. He'd sat here on so many afternoons that he had the map of scars memorized. The hearts and initials. The curses. The mindless doodles.

He took a deep breath and tried to clear his mind. But the itch from the cafeteria remained, an electric charge building in his fingertips. Humming up his arms and moving through his whole body.

Even here in his quiet place, encyclopedias and dictionaries and atlases surrounding him, Calvin could hear the whispers. He could see the premonitions flashing at him from the dust jackets wrapped around the thick books, the light reflecting off the protective plastic sleeves. They showed him paper cuts and broken toes. An earthquake shaking the heavy tomes right off their shelves and onto his skull. A domino of crashing bookcases that turned the whole library into a graveyard.

Calvin shut his eyes and put his head down on the desk, but it did nothing to get rid of the images. Nothing to keep the whispers from burrowing in.

Finally, Calvin reached into his backpack and pulled out a notebook. He let it thud against the desk and then set his pen down next to it.

He stared at the pen, not wanting to pick it up. But his fingers still itched, more intensely now than before. He hated doing it, but he knew it was the only way to silence the voices. His fingers curved around the pen while he flicked open his notebook with the other hand. He came to a white page and set the tip of the pen against it. He closed his eyes and let the whispers flood in, a soft muttering dragging him under and pulling him along.

He saw flashes of wild hair tangled in knots. The thing's restless eyes dripping with red tears. Its crimson lipstick clinging to its mouth like it'd just taken a long drink from someone's neck.

Calvin saw this demon's familiar face and the visions it spewed, cycling one after the other. His eyes snapped open, a blank look glazing them over, and his pen started scratching. It began filling the white pages with ink. With scenes too terrible to speak of.

He remembered that day five years ago, when everything

had changed. When he'd stood in front of that old mirror and whispered that name.

Bloody Mary.

He'd thought it was all a joke. But then something had tingled in his toes. A cold washing over him. Flooding into his lungs. Gripping his chest before it sank its claws into his heart, piercing him to the bone.

He'd nearly collapsed from the pain. And then the thing had appeared in front of him, filling the whole mirror. A vision that only he could see.

It had loomed over him, its face monstrous but still somehow beautiful. Its wicked grin was crowded with two rows of sharpened teeth. Its lips opened wide as if to devour him on the spot. Its bloodshot eyes lined with crimson kohl saw right through him, feasting on his every weakness, swallowing him in their ghastly depths.

He'd blinked and the demon had vanished. But he hadn't been able to shake that feeling of doom. Calamity waiting around every corner. The rules of Elena's game.

He was meant for death.

He thought his eyes had to be playing tricks on him, that it was just a made-up game. But the next morning, the visions had started. Terrible scenes had filled his head. Living nightmares that he couldn't ignore or wake up from. Catastrophes that he could only draw. That he was compelled to put to paper. That wouldn't stop.

Calvin's eyes fluttered and he came to. His fingers ached from squeezing the pen so tightly, but he felt a hundred times better. Empty. But the relief only lasted a moment as he glanced down at his creations, at the four pieces of paper he'd unconsciously pulled out of his notebook and filled with ink, the lines crisscrossing and connecting across the white space.

Four separate drawings of four dire scenes.

And then above it all, black lines flew off the pages, darkening the wooden desk, drawing all four pictures together under one monstrous umbrella, the demon's haunting face hunched over and looking on, reveling in the agony.

Calvin studied the images, a cold sweat trickling down the back of his neck, unsure of what he'd drawn. Of what it all meant. These felt different than his usual visions. More ominous. Like promises. He moved down the line and then paused over the last one. His fingers trembled as he lifted it, holding it close, making sure he hadn't missed something.

An ache quivered in his heart, and his mouth went suddenly dry. Then he opened his notebook and shoved all four pictures inside. He pushed away from the desk and scurried out of the stacks, swearing that the demon's eyes followed him as he went, taunting him over what was to come.

CHAPTER 3
STEPH

"Four."

Steph called for the set as she wound up, cocking her arm back, measuring out her approach. She took two steps and then leapt into the air, watching the volleyball ease into the setter's fingers, watching it jump right out like it'd taken a hop on a trampoline, watching as it sailed to the other side of the court, where the opposite hitter took a crack at it and hit it long.

She landed back on the ground, her shoes squeaking against the gym floor, and tried not to look disappointed.

"Good isolation, Steph," Coach Lee's voice called from the sideline as she clapped her hands together once. "That would have had the blockers fooled."

Steph smothered a grimace and nodded. Sure, she would have fooled the blockers. But she would have been able to hit around them, too. If she'd gotten the set.

She glared at their setter, who was in the center of the court, but Elena refused to meet her gaze. That was the sixth ball in a row that Elena had chosen not to send Steph's way. And as Steph got back in position to run the drill again, she started thinking it wasn't a coincidence.

"Four," Steph shouted, demanding the ball as the pass hung in the air, floating toward Elena. But one step into Steph's approach and Elena had already shaken her off, overcalling with a one and setting the ball quickly to their middle, who wasn't ready at all. Steph went through the motions, faking an attack, but she couldn't help watching the middle jump late. She couldn't avoid rolling her eyes as the girl sent the ball into the top of the net instead of to the wide-open court. Steph's frustration boiled over and her hands clenched into fists, but before she could use them, Coach Lee blew her whistle and called everyone in.

"That's it for today."

The freshman team gathered around their coach, taking squeezes from their water bottles as they listened.

"We've got some wrinkles to iron out, but we're on the right track for next week's match. And a particular shout-out to Elena for stepping in and taking over. It's not easy picking up the 5-1 system in just a week."

Elena beamed as the other girls cheered. It made Steph, who had shuffled to the back, want to throw up.

"And remember, I'll be choosing our captain soon. We'll

need someone who can pull the whole team together and really lead out there."

"That's got Elena's name all over it," Kayleigh, the middle hitter, who was also one of Elena's best friends, squealed. Again, Steph could feel her stomach turning. She had to take a long drink of water to stop herself from mouthing off.

"I've got my eye on a few potential captains," Coach Lee said, not giving anything away as she surveyed all her players. "Now get out of here. I'll see you all tomorrow."

And with that, the woman snapped up her clipboard and headed out, leaving the girls to chatter on their own as they packed their bags and peeled off their knee pads.

"You were so good today," one of the girls said to Elena as she sat down on the gym floor and began untying her shoes.

"Yeah. You're, like, already a boss out there," another girl tossed in. "Coach will definitely pick you."

"I mean, it'd be an honor to lead you all." Elena's cheeks reddened as if she were being modest, but Steph could see right through it.

"Don't you think the captain should be a team player?"

The words came out of Steph's mouth before she realized it.

"You don't think I'm a team player?" Elena didn't seem frazzled at all. In fact, she seemed to enjoy the chance at a confrontation.

"No. I don't."

Steph had to concentrate to get the words out, to deliver

them without letting her voice tremble. And after that, she didn't wait for Elena's reply. She grabbed her bag and took off, taking long strides across the floor and slamming through the gym doors. But she'd only made it a couple of steps before someone grabbed her elbow from behind and spun her around.

"What's the matter with you?" Elena snapped between angry huffs. "You can't talk to me like that."

And as Steph eyed the other girl, taking in her twitching eyes and red-hot cheeks, she had to wonder if anyone had ever stood up to her like this.

"Why not? Because it's the truth?" Steph tried her best to remain calm and levelheaded. "I'm the best hitter on the team—"

"And with Lindsay out for the season," Elena cut in, "I'm our *only* setter. You're a lot easier to replace than me."

The smirk on Elena's face couldn't have been more wicked if she'd planned Lindsay's freak tumble down the stairs and then stomped on the girl's wrist to make sure it was broken.

"Look, I don't know what your problem with me is," Steph started, "but you not setting me is just going to make us lose."

"We don't need you to win," Elena shot back, crossing her arms over her chest. "And once Coach makes me captain, I'll prove it."

"*If* she makes you captain."

Elena laughed right in Steph's face, and it was almost as bad as if she'd spit.

"You think the girls will want you as captain?" Elena clucked her tongue, leaning into the fake pity. "News flash: No one likes you. You're just a freaky-tall giant. Sasquatch Steph. Why don't you crawl back to the woods where you came from?"

Steph bristled and then shrank back. No one had ever come at her like that. No one had ever been so direct. Not that she hadn't known people called her names behind her back. She *was* tall. An anomaly at six feet and only fourteen years old. Her limbs were long and gangly and didn't look like they fit her body at all. And she was clumsy, tripping over her own big feet everywhere except on the volleyball court.

There, magically, she felt comfortable. Graceful, even. She felt like she belonged. And she wasn't about to give that up. Not without a fight.

"I'm not going anywhere," Steph said, stretching her spine up to her full height. "We'll just have to see who Coach Lee picks."

"As if you have a chance." But Elena didn't seem so sure now. And before Steph could get another word out, the girl spun and stalked back into the gym.

Steph's shoulders fell, unspooling from their tight knots. She'd talked a big game in front of Elena, but now the doubts started to creep in. If Coach Lee picked her for captain, could she really lead the team? The girls liked Elena more. They would listen to her, even if Steph was a better player, a more devoted one willing to put in the extra hours on the court, to dive after every ball that came her way. But would the other girls see that? Would they even care?

A rattling of wheels suddenly came up behind Steph, and she turned to see the night custodian pushing along her mop and bucket.

"Was that Elena?" the woman asked, pressing down on the brake on her janitor's cart and coming closer.

"Yes, Mom," Steph sighed, turning to face the woman. Seeing them together, they were unmistakable as mother and daughter. They had the same tall builds. The same untamable curls corkscrewing from their heads.

"It's nice to see you all are friends again."

"We were never friends," Steph shot back, her jaw clenching.

"You all used to spend every morning chattering away in the back seat."

"No, we didn't."

Steph would have remembered that, but her mom only shrugged. Then she wrapped her hands around the mop and pulled it out, dripping soapy water across the tiled lobby.

"You should get a start on your homework," Steph's mom said. "I've still got a couple of hours to go. But I made you a snack."

Steph nodded, and moseyed to the janitor's cart, pulling

out the brown paper sack her mom had brought. She opened it and spied two slices of homemade banana bread inside, her favorite.

"Thanks."

But Steph's mom had already walked out of earshot, humming to herself as she swirled the mop across the floor. Steph took a quick bite of the bread and then stuffed it back in the bag. She swallowed and turned to head off to the library, but something caught her eye.

Her reflection in the soapy mop water.

She stopped and bent over the bucket to look closer, studying her features—her sweaty forehead and the stray spirals of hair that had come out of her ponytail during practice. Did that girl really have what it took to go toe-to-toe with Elena? To beat her out for captain?

Steph sighed and shook her head.

Maybe if she weren't such a giant. If the other girls liked her like they did Elena.

Then, as Steph stared down at her own face, it began to change, shifting into something softer. Something more delicate. A face she'd tried her best to forget. But no matter how many times she blinked or rubbed her eyes, the vision remained. It came into focus until Steph's knees trembled underneath her, her heart leaping into her throat.

But she'd buried that—those feelings. She was already different enough. A giant. Sasquatch Steph. She didn't need to add to the name-calling. She didn't need to make things harder on her mother or herself.

Steph swayed on her feet. But then she snapped herself out of it. And before she could fall under its spell again, she lunged forward and kicked the cart.

Water sloshed all over the floor, and the reflection disappeared. Then Steph turned and rushed toward the library, her gym bag clutched tight to her pounding chest.

CHAPTER 4
ELENA

The water ran warm from the faucet, pooling in Elena's cupped hands. She splashed it against her face, lightly massaging her skin with her fingertips. The water droplets tickled as they slid off her nose. She dipped her hands back into the sink and repeated the ritual, carefully patting her face dry with a fluffy towel. She studied her reflection in the mirror, her cheeks clean and pink from the face wash, her skin unblemished. She reached into the vanity cabinet and pulled out a jar of moisturizer.

A dab on her forehead. A streak down her nose. She smeared it across each cheekbone and then left a dot on her chin. She began rubbing it all in, the cream cooling her skin. Keeping it smooth. Keeping her beautiful.

Her phone suddenly dinged on the counter and Elena's eyes flickered to it. She saw the text message but ignored it, turning back to gaze at her reflection instead.

She tilted her head this way and that, puckering her lips and sucking in her cheeks, trying to catch the light until—there. Her hands floated up, fingertips trailing lightly over her skin. She locked eyes with her reflection, getting lost in the image, the way her whole face seemed to glow. She looked radiant. Irresistible. Like she was an angel. Or Aphrodite herself.

A smile blossomed on Elena's lips right as her phone chimed again. But this time, even though something whispered in her ear to keep staring, she was able to pull away from the mirror. She looked down at her phone and tapped on the screen. She figured it was a message from one of her girlfriends. Or maybe Henry. But as Elena slid the message open, she was surprised to see that it was from a number she didn't know.

Hi, beautiful.

Elena stared at the message, wondering who had sent it. Was it serious or just some stupid dare? She had a boyfriend. Whoever this was had to know that. She wasn't in the market for a new one. She and Henry were coming up on their anniversary. Three years together. She'd had a crush on him ever since she was nine years old. And in the sixth grade, when they'd finally started going out, she'd known that they'd be together forever. She'd known that they were soulmates.

Elena's finger hovered over the message to delete it, but the screen flickered suddenly and an onslaught of messages came pouring in.

Rose after rose after rose. A string of them filling her screen.

A giggle bubbled out of Elena, and she clapped her hand over her mouth, surprised at the odd fluttering in her stomach. She scrolled down, counting the emojis until she got to a dozen. It was a sweet gesture, even if it was a bit creepy. But it was also flattering. And mysterious. Elena waited a few beats before giving in.

> Who is this?

She held her breath, her bottom lip caught between her teeth.

> An admirer.

Elena snorted. She knew better than to fall for that.

> And not a weirdo, I promise.

She rolled her eyes and slid her phone into her pajama pocket. She knew these types of guys. And they were definitely weirdos—some nerd on the math team or in the marching band. She would kill whichever of her friends had given her number out to some loser.

As Elena made her way down the hallway to her room, she

thought about Henry. Her boyfriend and soulmate. She'd had a crush on him for as long as she could remember. Ever since—

Her eyes flitted to the closed door at the end of the hall, and it was like a hook had snagged in her heart, reeling her in. A soft music filled her ears and beckoned her forward. She passed by her room and kept going, sleepwalking as she turned the knob and opened the door to her grandmother's old room.

She moved to the middle of the room, leaving the door open so that light filtered in from the hallway. She couldn't remember the last time she'd been in here, but so little had changed. Had it really been five years since her grandmother had passed away? She walked over to the dresser and rifled through the trinkets there. She picked through a couple of bracelets and a pair of earrings, but none of it was anything she'd want to wear now. It was all so old, the silver tarnished and the gems cloudy. And that wasn't all. Her hand cut through the stack of books and pulled out a thicker tome. A volume of fairy tales.

Carefully, Elena brushed the dust off the cover and opened the book. The spine cracked as she flipped through it, and Elena remembered how her grandmother used to read to her. She didn't remember the stories, though, and she only half recognized the illustrations. She squinted and tried to make out the words, but she quickly realized that they weren't written in English. Her grandmother must have translated as she read. Or known the stories by heart. Elena kept turning the pages, and then an illustration made her stop.

A beautiful woman stood in front of a mirror. But her reflection hid something monstrous: a demon with glowing eyes and bloody lips. Something about that image tugged at the back of Elena's mind. She looked closely at the page and tried to make out the title of this particular story.

"Die Verflucht Frau."

Of course, she didn't know what the German meant, but she could look it up. As she reached into her pocket to take out her phone, a chill crept up her neck. Goose bumps scattered along the backs of her arms and a strange draft gusted through the room, grabbing the pages of the book and turning them so that the woman and the mirror disappeared from sight.

Don't you have more important things to do?

Elena looked over her shoulder. There'd been someone standing there behind her, she could have sworn. But it was only her reflection. Her face bathed in the pale moonlight streaming in through the window.

Come and take a closer look.

Something beckoned to Elena, and she forgot about the fairy tale book. She took a few steps until she was standing right in front of the antique mirror, with its lacquered wood and inset pearls. And in this light she noticed a silvery swirl running all the way around the oval glass, a filigree of symbols that could have been the constellations in the night sky.

Look at how beautiful you are.

Elena's eyes snapped up to her moonlit features, her skin soft and pale. Her eyes were clear and gray, bottomless.

A face like that deserves the world.

Elena nodded, wholly entranced by her reflection, the way the glass rippled, as if she could step right through it into another world.

Deserves everything she wants.

In the mirror, Elena saw herself reaching into her pajama pocket. Saw herself pulling out her phone, smiling as she read a new message.

She blinked and looked down, surprised to find her phone there in her hands. The screen pulsed in her palm and she saw that her admirer had sent her more messages.

You don't have to be creeped out.

I would talk to you at school, but I don't want to make Henry jealous.

Does he ever tell you how beautiful you are?

Does he ever buy you flowers or chocolates?

Does he know how lucky he is to be with you?

Are you still there, Elena?

As Elena stared at the screen, she couldn't keep the grin off her face. This feeling of being wanted—it was powerful. It was intoxicating. Should she write back? Just to learn who he was? She liked the attention. She liked the compliments. And Henry would never find out.

Elena looked at the mirror, studying her reflection one last time, those words echoing in her head.

You deserve the world.

And she did.

> I'm still awake.

She looked at her message for a second and then hit send, turning her back on the mirror as she made her way out of the room. She shut the door behind her, so wrapped up in thinking about her secret admirer's identity that she failed to notice that someone was watching her. Something. Its face pressed right up to the mirror, staring out at her retreating back, a wicked smile curling its bloody lips.

CHAPTER 5
GRACE

With a sharp *thwack*, the ball sailed through the air and smacked into the gym floor. In the stands, Grace slid to the edge of her seat, ready to leap up in celebration. But she quickly shook her head and slumped back as the ref blew her whistle and waved her flag high, signaling that the hit had gone long.

The next point. They'd definitely get that one. And then they'd have clinched the first set, halfway to victory. Grace nibbled on the end of her nail as she watched the scoreboard change, the visitors creeping closer. It was now 24–23. Jennings High needed to win this set point or it'd be all tied up.

Grace held her breath as the opposing team served the ball. She watched it float over the net, ready to be passed and set and put away. But their player wobbled underneath the serve. Hesitating, she shanked the ball into the sidelines. The whistle blew again, the ref waved her flag, and just like that, the score was tied.

On the floor, Elena barked out threats, furious that her teammate would miss something so easy. The whistle blew and the visitors served in another ball. But this time the home team managed to get the pass-off. And it was right to Elena, who set it perfectly for their middle hitter.

It was a lightning-fast attack, but the opposing middle had read it. She was there, her arms soaring over the net, blocking off the shot and sending it rocketing right back to the home side of the court.

Instinctively, Elena dove to the side, but she wasn't the only player going for the ball. With a terrible crash, Elena collided with Steph. Their heads bashed against each other with an awful clunking sound. Their arms tangled together, wrenched into awkward angles.

This time, Grace did jump to her feet, leaning toward the court, almost losing her balance and tumbling down the bleachers. Her fingers dipped underneath her collar and she fished out her locket, holding it tightly against her lips, stretching the thin silver chain. The locket quivered in her mouth as she watched the aftermath, the coaches and players running onto the court while the two girls lay there. Unmoving. Not making a sound.

Out of the corner of her eye, Grace spotted Henry flying through the stands, his shoes screeching as he hit the gym floor,

41

racing toward his downed girlfriend. Grace felt an instinctive urge to do the same. But she knew Elena wouldn't want her there. She would only call her names for caring. Freak. Or stalker. They weren't friends anymore. They hadn't been for a very long time.

Grace planted herself in the stands, her eyes straining to see what was happening as her heart pounded, praying the girls were all right—that Elena wasn't seriously injured.

A few seconds passed, and then Elena's arms moved. Her head lifted slowly and she sat up straight. A dazed look clouded her eyes, but then as she turned and saw Steph's curls on the floor next to her, her gaze narrowed into a murderous glare.

"I'm fine."

Grace could read Elena's lips from the stands as she got to her feet and pushed everyone away. She turned her back on her fallen teammate, rolling her shoulders and wrists. Checking that her knees still worked. She didn't give Steph a second glance. Didn't offer her a hand up. But Steph managed to collect herself on her own. She got to her feet, rubbing the spot on her head where the girls had collided. No one really seemed to notice, though, as Elena took center stage, shooting the crowd a thumbs-up and getting back into position, barking orders, trying to get the team pumped up. They were down now. They couldn't afford to lose this next point.

The locket slipped from Grace's lips. She relaxed but didn't sit back down. No one in the bleachers did as they watched the next point—the ball served in and passed cleanly, Elena trying to dump it over on the second touch. But the sneaky play didn't fool their opponents. The visitors dove for the ball and got it up. They were able to run an in-system play off the dig and put the ball away easily, taking the first set.

The crowd groaned and Elena slammed the ball into the gym floor, turning her back on her team and stalking off to the locker room. She wasn't alone, however, as Steph signaled to their coach and went after her.

A queasiness rocked Grace's stomach as everyone around her sat back down. In the absence of play, she suddenly felt very much alone. Her head tilted around and she saw Henry sidling through the crowd, stepping from bleacher to bleacher as he took his place back with his friends. The popular crowd.

Grace turned away from them. The high fives, shoulder bumps, and roaring laughter only made her feel more out of place. Like she didn't belong. What was she doing here? What part of her had thought it was a good idea to come to the volleyball match all by herself? Being there didn't make her cool. In fact, it made her look sad and desperate. It let everyone know that she was alone.

Ears burning, Grace sat back, hoping to hide in all the other hunched bodies. But right as she hit the hard plank of the bleacher, her eyes caught sight of someone. Someone staring right at her.

Calvin. Also sitting alone. Only he had taken up residence at the very top of the stands, his notebook open on his lap, his fingers curled around a pen, ink staining the side of his hand.

But he wasn't drawing. Just staring, unblinking, right at Grace. He was staring so intently that she couldn't sit still.

She shot to her feet and moved across the bleachers. When she got to the end of her row, she took one last look at Calvin—who by this point had turned back to his notebook—and hurried in the opposite direction.

Luckily, the concessions stand was that way, so Grace didn't feel like a complete weirdo. But as she moved out of sight, she started to wonder if Calvin really had been looking at her or if it was just her imagination running wild, making her believe what she dreamed of at night.

Her whole face flared with the thought, an entirely different kind of embarrassment scorching her cheeks. She got in line and shuffled forward, grabbing a box of popcorn and paying without looking up. But as she turned to head back to the bleachers, she ran smack into someone's chest.

Popcorn flew as the box crunched like an accordion between them. An apology spilled out of her mouth as she tried to make sure she hadn't smashed any butter or oil onto the boy's shirt with its picture of an old-school werewolf.

Grace froze then and looked up.

"You've seen *The Wolf Man?*" The question was voiced before she could think better of it. "You like creature features?"

"Creature features?" Calvin asked, sounding completely confused. But Grace wouldn't let that deter her. She had on her Bride of Frankenstein shirt today, the monster's black hair set in a stiff cylinder, white lightning bolts running up each side, looking like some kind of demon sister to Nefertiti—a queen in her own right.

"Come on." Grace hoped she didn't sound too crazed. "That's the Wolf Man there on your shirt."

"This?" And Calvin pulled out his shirt to look at the design. "This is just something my mom got for me."

Grace frowned, unable to hide her disappointment.

"Well, actually," Calvin added, sheepish all of a sudden. "It's something she made for me. She got it from one of my sketches. It was kind of a cool birthday surprise."

And just like that, Grace was back, the drawing she'd found burning a hole in her pocket. Because of course she had the demon illustration she'd found on the stairwell with her. She'd carried it around the whole week. Should she ask about it now? It wasn't like he knew she had it. He might not even know he'd lost it.

Or maybe he'd left it behind for her. Maybe he'd seen her looking at him that day in the hallway and drawn it just for her. She wanted to show him, but she also knew how stalker-y that might seem.

"So are you here by yourself?" Grace changed direction, feeling confident suddenly. Hoping that maybe he'd want to watch the second set with her. "I didn't know you came to these."

"My mom's the coach," Calvin replied, shrugging, a fact that Grace hadn't realized. "I've been coming to games since I was a kid. That top bleacher might as well have my name on it."

"She still makes you come?"

"She doesn't like leaving me at home by myself." Calvin half smiled, his eyes suddenly zoning out, darting over her shoulder for a few seconds before he refocused.

"Are you okay?" Grace asked. His hands had started trembling and one side of his face had contracted into a wince.

"I'm fine," Calvin assured her, but his expression only got more pained. "It's just a headache. I get these kind of migraine things every now and then."

"Can I get you something?" Grace wanted to reach out and still his shaking hands. Or set her cool palm against his forehead. But she kept to herself as he waved her worry away, forcing a smile through his obvious discomfort.

"I just need to lie down for a bit."

And then, before Grace could say anything else, Calvin dashed away, leaving her alone, a battlefield of fallen popcorn puffs lying at her feet. Slowly, Grace turned around, looking behind her as if she might see what had caused Calvin's sudden sickness, but it was only the popcorn machine, the glass reflecting a greasy, distorted image back at her.

Even the shy boys can't stand to be near you.

Grace shook her head, but her murky reflection didn't follow suit. Its eyes glowed instead, turning into bloodred rubies.

They should make a monster movie about you. About all the boys you've scared away.

The popcorn maker suddenly ground to life, rattling as fresh kernels exploded out of its mouth like firecrackers.

Grace stuttered backward, blinking at her reflection in the glass, her eyes back to normal. She held her gaze for another second and then snapped around, heading for the exit, her phone already out to message her dad that she needed him to pick her up early. But she wasn't watching where she was going. She didn't see the girl coming out of the locker room. She didn't hear her giggles, the way she held her tongue between her teeth as she tried to cover up her excitement. Grace veered away at the last second and managed to only clip the girl, but the glancing blow was enough to send both of their phones clattering to the ground.

"Watch it," Elena snarled, the laughter leeched from her voice.

Grace paled, not looking up as she scurried across the gym floor in pursuit of Elena's phone. She couldn't believe her luck. First Calvin and now this. She prayed the screen hadn't cracked.

"Here, I've got it," Grace began, but another pair of athletic shoes had come through the locker room's swinging doors.

"Drop something?"

Steph dangled the phone in front of them, and Grace felt

like she might spontaneously combust from Elena's death-ray glare. Whatever words they'd exchanged in that locker room must have been intense.

"Give it to me." Elena pushed Grace out of the way, her hand outstretched. But right then, a new message popped up on the screen for all three girls to see.

A boy's torso flashed in front of them, some headless body in swim trunks flexing his chest and abs for the camera. Grace couldn't help but gasp, which she was sure only made Elena madder. But Elena didn't say anything or even look at them as she snatched the phone away from Steph and stormed back onto the court, Steph following a few beats behind her, leaving Grace there by herself.

But even as Grace hurried outside to meet her dad, she couldn't help thinking about what she'd seen. She recognized that giggle now. The one she'd heard before her collision with Elena. It was the telltale sound of flirtation. Of a girl in love. She had never received those kinds of messages from a boy, but that hadn't stopped her from imagining them, from feeling those same bubbles fizzing in her stomach.

However, something worried her at the back of her brain. Something it didn't take her long to realize. That headless boy who had popped up on Elena's phone—it definitely wasn't the girl's boyfriend. It wasn't Henry.

CHAPTER 6
STEPH

"I'll have dinner ready in a half hour," Steph's mom promised as they walked into the house. "Think you can wait that long? Your aunt Ellen's dropping your brother off."

"No problem," Steph replied as she dropped her gym bag by the door. "I've got homework anyways."

"Take an apple to snack on."

Steph's mom opened the fridge, which looked pretty bare, and took out the last piece of fruit. Steph felt guilty accepting it. But she was hungry, so she took it, wishing there was something more she could do to help out around the house.

"You were great tonight, honey," Steph's mom said proudly.

And Steph had to take a bite of the apple to hide her smile. Her mom had missed the first half of the match, but she'd finished with her mopping and cleaning up in time to catch the end, when Steph had been better than good. When she'd been phenomenal. Somehow, she'd shifted into another gear. Unlocked a new skill level. It'd started with a couple of ace serves. And then she had thrown up a few stuffed solo blocks. Even Elena had admitted that Steph had a hot hand, and had begrudgingly started to set her, Steph's kill total climbing to her season high as she hit over four hundred.

She'd led them to victory. And she could still feel the girls crowded around her at the end, patting her on the shoulder and giving her hugs. Acknowledging that she had the stuff. Noticing her for the first time.

"If you keep this up, you might even get a scholarship." Steph's mom beamed at her as she got out a pot and a box of pasta. "Which is why homework is important. So go. I'll call you when dinner is ready."

And Steph made her way out of the kitchen. As she passed through the living room, which her mom had converted into a third bedroom where she slept, Steph could hear her mother running the faucet and humming to herself. It was a small house with thin walls, which didn't leave much room for privacy. But they made do. Having the room at the end of the hall helped, even if it was tiny.

Wedging the apple between her front teeth, Steph pushed her bedroom door open and slipped inside. She unshouldered her backpack and let it thud against the floor. Then she followed it down, plopping into the only chair the room had to offer. She took another bite of the apple and set the rest down on the corner of her desk. She closed her eyes and concentrated on her chewing, the apple quickly turning to sweet mush in her mouth. She rolled her shoulders back and stretched her fingers. She cocked her wrists. She was definitely going to feel that match in the morning. The soreness in her muscles and the tightness in her joints. She'd probably have a bruise on her hip, too, from when she dove after that ball and collided with Elena.

Elena.

While Steph felt she had won over most of her teammates with her stellar play that night, she knew she'd only made things worse with their setter. When the girl had stormed off after they lost that first set, Steph had gone after her without really thinking.

At first she'd thought she could calm her down. Elena was the only setter they had, and that meant that they needed her on the court and in a good headspace if they had any chance at winning. But when Steph had swung into the locker room and seen the girl on her phone texting away, something had finally snapped in her.

She'd yelled at Elena. Right there in their locker room. She hadn't held one thing back. She'd spelled out exactly why they were losing, that it was all Elena's fault because she refused to set their best hitter. She'd barely gotten Steph the ball the entire first set. They had to play as a team if they wanted to win. And teamwork started with Elena letting go of whatever petty grudge she had against Steph.

Unsurprisingly, Steph's outburst hadn't gone over well. But Elena hadn't called her anything she hadn't already heard. More rounds of Sasquatch Steph. Freak. Giraffe Girl. Steph had managed to weather it all, at least to Elena's face. And that seemed to have made Elena even angrier. She'd practically shoved Steph into the lockers. Then she'd turned back to her phone and kept right on texting, actually giggling as she left Steph behind.

But when Steph had walked back onto that court, she'd realized she couldn't wait around to be handed her chance to shine. She had to take it for herself. She had to go after her serves and attack every free ball. She had to jump higher and stretch her arms farther. She had to play every point like it was set point. No excuses. No letting up. And somehow, it'd actually worked.

Steph opened her eyes and stared at her reflection in the small mirror propped up on her desk. Her hair was even crazier than usual, the curls flying all over the place, her face still splotched from the match, her long neck sprouting high from her collarbones. But for once, she didn't feel strange. She didn't feel like an alien or a freak. She felt like a winner.

Her eyes flicked to the wall, to the plaque and medal hanging there—Rookie of the Year and Tournament Champion. They were the only trophies she'd ever won. She'd only started playing volleyball that summer, for a local club team. Her mom had signed her up so she wouldn't be home alone all day. Steph hadn't taken it seriously at first, not until she'd realized she had a knack for the game. She'd found her footing out there on the court. She felt strong when she played—sure of herself. She was the first to sign up for the freshman team when Coach Lee had posted tryouts earlier that year. Volleyball had given her confidence. It had given her something that she was not just good at—but great at. Something that might even help her family.

If she could get a scholarship, then she could go to college for free. And even though that was still four years away, she got goose bumps thinking about it. She just had to keep playing like she had today. And also keep her grades up. Which reminded her . . .

Steph leaned over and unzipped her backpack, pulling out her history textbook.

Her whole desk rattled as she dropped the thick volume on it. Grabbing a pencil, Steph opened her notebook and read through the essay prompt. Something about the first American colonies. She read through the question again and flipped through her textbook.

As her eyes traveled over the words, she couldn't help but feel distracted. It was like a gentle breeze had whipped up in the back of her mind. Soft and subtle. Haunting.

She tried to shake the feeling. She tried to focus on the textbook. But it persisted.

The strange echoes insisted she listen. So Steph looked up from the book and did just that.

Only, nothing came to her. The feeling had left, gone as suddenly as it had arrived. Steph waited another second and turned back to her textbook. But this time something caught her eye. A twinkle of light glinting off the medal hanging on her wall. And when she looked, the light shined off her plaque, its reflection almost blinding her. Then she saw a flash of another world. Another room. Another girl. And she heard it. The whisper breaking through.

Beautiful, isn't she?

Steph leaned forward, getting a closer look at the girl, at her short hair and bent head, the pencil tucked behind her ear as she concentrated on something in her lap.

She knew this girl without having ever met her. She'd seen her in dreams. Peered at her in the edges of mirrors. Looked for her across the volleyball court, hoping to find her on the opposing team. She'd searched for her ever since she'd seen her face in Elena's grandmother's mirror five years ago.

Soulmates.

Steph startled at that word, at its implication.

There's no point in fighting it.

Steph shook her head. She didn't need to fight it because it wasn't true.

It's who you are.

No. It wasn't. It couldn't be.

What are you so afraid of? Disappointing your mother? Alienating your teammates?

Steph's hands flew to her ears and she tried to block out the voice, the venomous thoughts seeping in.

Being more of a freak than you already are?

"No," Steph shouted, jolting forward in her chair, heart pounding as if she'd woken from a nightmare.

A trickle of sweat slipped down the back of her neck as she sneaked a glance at the plaque. But the window was gone, the metal cold steel again. And she suddenly couldn't tell if she'd been dreaming.

"Steph," her mom called from the kitchen, interrupting the girl's racing thoughts. "Dinnertime. Come wash up so we can say grace."

Steph's hands trembled as she took a last tentative peek at the plaque. The metal flashed again, but this time it brought her a different vision. A horrible one. A woman with bloody lips and weeping eyes. A wicked grin that threatened to swallow her whole.

Steph lurched back and almost fell out of her chair, but the vision had already vanished, there and gone so quickly that she'd hardly had time to register it.

She sat there, rubbing her eyes. She must just be tired from the game—seeing things that weren't there, daydreaming about a girl who didn't exist. She couldn't like her even if she did exist.

But what if she could?

Steph quickly shoved that thought away. Gulping it down deep. Locking it where it couldn't see the light of day.

CHAPTER 7
ELENA

This was it.

Elena could feel it in her bones. Coaches didn't just call their players out of class in the middle of the day for nothing. And why shouldn't she get it? She'd turned the game around last night. She'd led the team to victory—ran the offense on her own and racked up a record number of assists in the process.

She'd kept them from losing. Which was all she could think as she hurried across the gym, ignoring the game of pickup basketball that a group of upperclassmen had going on the court.

When she got to Coach Lee's office door, she paused, pulling out her phone to check her hair and makeup in the front camera.

No one deserves this more than you.

They didn't.

You earned this. You're the best.

And she was.

A satisfied smile curved her lips inward as she reached out and knocked, rushing to open the door and peeking her head in before she got a response.

"You wanted to see me?" Elena asked, looking across the office at Coach Lee.

"Come on in, Elena," the woman said. "Have a seat."

Elena slid forward and quickly took one of the two empty chairs there in front of the coach's desk. She set her bag down and folded her hands in her lap, but she couldn't stay still. Her knees bounced and her eyes darted all over. She caught sight of a cute little boy peeking around the edge of a picture frame, and was surprised to realize it was Calvin, proudly showing off his missing two front teeth. She sometimes forgot that he was Coach Lee's son. But then, she hadn't been *Coach* Lee back in their carpool days. Only *Mrs.* Lee.

Elena's eyes flickered away and landed on the giant case behind the desk. The huge sheet of glass glared in the office's fluorescent light, revealing row upon row of shiny plaques and medals, trophies of all sizes—the biggest of which had to be almost as tall as Elena.

"We got that for coming in second at states," Coach Lee remarked, causing Elena to blink. She hadn't realized she'd been staring so intently. "You should have seen the one the champions got."

Elena swallowed her laugh, unsure if Coach Lee was trying to make a joke or not.

"Have you ever won it all?" Elena scooted forward in her chair and sat up straighter.

"Unfortunately not." Coach Lee leaned back, her face tilted up as she seemed to remember. "Second was as close as we ever got."

She paused then, as if considering whether she should share more or not. Then she went on, speaking softer now, as if she were giving away some priceless secret.

"That year was special. It was the best group of seniors I've ever had. They'd been playing together since they were freshmen and had developed an unbelievable chemistry. It was like they could read each other's minds. They always knew where to be and who was getting set. They were seamless out there on the court."

Coach Lee set her elbows on the desk and met Elena's gaze.

"But they didn't start out that way. They grew into that team. They grew into each other. It wasn't easy, though. They needed a strong leader to pull them together."

Elena bit her bottom lip to try to keep her excitement in check. She could feel it coming now. The reason she'd been called here in the first place.

"I was impressed with what I saw the other night," Coach Lee went on. "How you played when our backs were against the wall. You didn't give up. Which is something I look for in my players. Something I look for when I'm picking the team captain."

Elena couldn't keep it in any longer. The words burst out of her.

"Coach, I'm so honored and so ready—"

But right then, a knock came at the door. Elena whipped around in her chair, annoyed at the interruption. Had those upperclassmen popped their basketball or something? Had one of them broken a leg?

The door opened a crack and a familiar curly head poked inside.

"You wanted to see me?"

At the sight of Steph, all the blood drained from Elena's face.

"Come in and have a seat." Coach Lee motioned for Steph to take the chair next to Elena. "I was just telling Elena how impressed I was with her play last night."

Steph nodded as she sat down.

"I was very impressed with your play, too." Coach Lee sent the words in Steph's direction. "The two of you really stepped up. And you worked together, which is what impressed me most."

Elena could feel Steph's eyes searching for hers, but she refused to turn and meet her gaze. Refused to acknowledge her teammate, the girl who was stealing her spotlight.

"As I was saying to Elena before you got here," Coach Lee

continued, clearly ignoring the tension that had crept into the room. Or maybe she was oblivious to it. "The best team I ever coached was a group of seniors who played like they were family. They were so close. So in sync. They made it all the way to the state finals."

Coach Lee left off, letting her words sink in for a moment, as if they were the most important she'd spoken so far.

"I think you all could be that team. In three years. Or maybe even two. You've got the talent and the drive to win. With some strong leadership, you could go all the way."

Elena, who had been fidgeting in her chair, suddenly grew still. This was it. One of them would be captain. And it'd better be her.

"That's why I want you *both* to be captains this year."

Coach Lee's announcement hung in the air, a free ball waiting to be played.

"*Two* captains?" Elena choked out. She hadn't expected that. It was almost worse than losing out to Steph altogether.

"Co-captains," Coach Lee specified, sweeping her hands together across her desk as if that would unite the two girls. Maybe she wasn't as oblivious as Elena thought.

As the coach continued talking, Elena found herself losing focus.

She was going to be a co-captain? With Steph?

She sneaked a side glance at the girl next to her. At least Steph didn't seem that happy about it either. Elena blinked and looked away, zoning out in the glare of the trophy case, noticing her faded reflection there behind Coach Lee. An angel hovering over one shoulder. Steph, the devil, on the other.

Thief!

The mirror Elena opened her mouth wide and bared her teeth in a silent scream. Her head flickered from side to side and she tore at her blonde hair.

You deserve this. Not her. She stole this from you.

The words slithered in her ears, venomous but true.

You can't let her do this. You can't let her win. What will she take from you next?

"Elena?"

Her name pulled her back into focus, but that last thought lingered in Elena's head. She glanced at the trophy case again and saw only her reflection, her hair perfectly straight, her mouth closed in concentration.

"What do you say?" Coach Lee asked.

"I can't wait to lead alongside Steph," Elena replied, trying her best to sell it. She didn't have any other choice. Not yet, at least. "We'll make a great team."

Elena turned to face Steph, plastering on a smile, covering up her disappointment and the anger seething in her stomach like acid. Luckily, the school bell rang just then, letting Elena jump to her feet and grab her stuff without seeming rude.

"I've got a quiz next period," she explained quickly, knowing no one would call her bluff. "See you at practice."

She had her backpack on and was out the door before any-one could say anything. But as she stomped down the hallway, she heard Steph calling her name. Elena ignored her and kept going. But Steph had freakishly long legs that caught up to her in a hurry.

"Hey, we should talk—"

"There's nothing to talk about." Elena finally stopped and whipped around so quickly that Steph almost collided with her. "I deserved this and you took it from me. I hope you're happy."

"I didn't—"

But Elena cut Steph off with a snarl, and the girl actually stuttered backward, like Elena had fangs. Like she was some-thing to be afraid of.

Good. She should be afraid.

"Just stay out of my way."

And Elena stormed off, satisfied when Steph didn't come after her. She was light-headed and could feel a fever rising in her face. Her cheeks had probably turned bright red, too. Not cute at all. She needed space, a moment to gather her thoughts. Or maybe she needed to just scream her lungs raw.

Getting to her locker, Elena spun the dial and pulled it open in record time. She set her phone down on top of a stack of text-books and then shoved her whole head in, letting out a silent scream.

She didn't know what she'd done to deserve something as insulting as a co-captaincy. Didn't Coach Lee think she could handle it on her own? Hadn't Coach Lee seen her playing her heart out the other night? Leading their team to victory? Elena had done everything right, and still she was being punished. This was so impossibly unfair. So beyond embarrassing—

Elena's thoughts broke off as her phone lit up underneath her chin. She glanced down, and excitement came over her, shivering through her whole body.

It was her anonymous admirer again. More roses. Only this time it was a photo of a bouquet of them and not only the emoji.

Elena's whole face flushed as she thought about him, this mysterious boy who she'd been texting with for the past week. No matter how many times she told herself she was done texting him, the mystery of him and his compliments drew her back in. She'd studied that shirtless photo for hours, and still she couldn't figure out who he was. An upperclassman, definitely. And a hot one, at that. But which one? Her mind filled with the possibilities, flipping through them all like some kind of dating scrapbook.

Maybe it was one of the seniors on the baseball team. Or Milton, the junior class president. She swore she'd seen him looking her way in the cafeteria the other day. Or it could be one of the guys from the varsity soccer team. A group of them had come out to watch their volleyball game last night.

A smile bubbled on her lips and Elena's fingers flew to respond. But right as she hit send and glanced up to the mirror in her locker, she saw it.

Bloodshot eyes. Wild hair. A crazed expression.

A demon.

Elena startled backward.

"You okay?" Henry asked, chuckling as Elena turned to face him, her eyes wide. "I didn't mean to scare you."

She checked the mirror again, only seeing her boyfriend in the reflection now. That kind, gentle face that she knew so well. She tried to shake off the bad feeling. She must have been imagining things.

"I'm all right," Elena said, touching his shoulder as she quickly flipped her phone over. She felt it warm with a new message, but she didn't look. She'd have to get back to her anonymous admirer later. "Walk me to class?"

CHAPTER 8
CALVIN

Calvin sat on a bench in the lobby watching the rest of the student body flow past. Usually in the midst of so many people, he'd worry. He'd get that itching in his fingertips, the images scratching at the back of his head, trying to claw their way out.

But it never bothered him here, with the students slipping past so quickly, caught in the mad dash of an afternoon escape. His classmates were there and gone. The visions didn't have a chance to take hold. It left Calvin at peace, his notebook shut, his mind clear, uninterrupted, watching the heads as they bobbed along until—

"Grace!" He called her name without thinking and then watched as she paused in the middle of the lobby, a boulder in the stream. She wore a confused look as her head swiveled around.

"Over here." Calvin waved and she finally spotted him, her eyes opening wide. She actually pinched her arm before snapping to and walking over.

"You okay?" Calvin asked, giving her a concerned look.

"Yeah. Fine. Just had an itch." Grace flushed as she stuttered through the words. "What's up?"

She hovered over him, her hands clasped in front of her like in prayer. She looked nervous. Unsure.

But then why wouldn't she wonder? Other than their brief encounter at the volleyball game the other night, they hadn't talked in forever. Calvin had barely noticed her—or anyone, for that matter—in the years since their carpool days. He'd always kept his distance. Kept to himself.

But something had changed. Something was coming.

The four drawings pulsed in his notebook, tucked away safely but always with him. The ones he had drawn in the library. A series. Unlike any of his other pictures. Visions that he couldn't figure out. At least, not yet.

And Grace—she was in them. She was tied to it, too. She could be the answer.

"I watched that movie," Calvin replied, after a moment of silence. "*The Wolf Man.*"

She looked at him blankly for a second, and he rushed to fill the awkward break, pushing his glasses up his nose nervously. He wasn't used to talking so much. He wasn't used to putting himself out there.

"It took me forever to find online, but it was actually pretty good. Once I got used to the black and white."

"You watched it?"

"Yeah."

And with that one word, a dam opened up somewhere inside Grace, a flood of excited words rushing out of her mouth.

"Weren't the special effects so good? The hair and makeup. The way they did the transformation at the end. I mean, I know it looks a little cheesy by today's standards, but it was way ahead of its time. Advanced even for 1941."

He could practically see her geek heart pounding out of her chest.

"It was cool," Calvin said, which worked to slow her down as she took a deep breath.

"I can't believe you actually watched it."

This time she mumbled it under her breath and Calvin did his best to pretend like he hadn't heard.

"So are you heading home?"

She nodded. "Taking the bus. You?"

"I'm sticking around." Calvin tilted his head back toward the gym. The doors were open and he could hear the volleyball team warming up, gym shoes squeaking and open palms smacking against the balls. "My mom's got practice."

"You just sit there and watch them play?"

Calvin shrugged. "It isn't that bad. I manage to keep busy."

A beat passed between them, and Calvin figured that'd be the end of their conversation. Grace had a bus to catch.

"Do you want some company?"

Grace surprised him with the offer, and then did her best to avoid eye contact.

"What about your bus?"

"My dad can pick me up when he gets off work."

"Well, if you're sure it's not a problem," Calvin said.

Grace smiled giddily as she followed Calvin into the gym, practically skipping behind him, and Calvin found that he was actually happy to have a companion. They skirted around the court, watching the players as they stretched and loosened up their shoulders, some of them taping their fingers while others slid knee pads onto their legs. Calvin walked to mid-court and mounted the bleachers, climbing up to the top row before plopping down.

"I usually hang out up here," Calvin said, getting comfortable. He set his notebook down beside him as he waited for Grace to join.

"Don't they think it's weird? You watching them practice?" Grace seemed unsure as she lowered herself onto the bleacher, her eyes flicking between him and the girls on the court.

"They don't even notice me," Calvin assured her.

And then, because he wanted to get her mind off the girls, he shot out the first question that popped into his head.

"So are you, like, really into Halloween?"

She giggled, her head dipping to look at her shirt, which featured a monster that Calvin didn't recognize. Something with slimy green scales and gills and fangs.

"It's kind of my thing," Grace replied shyly. "I really love spooky stuff. Monster movies and haunted houses. The creepier, the better."

She looked like she had something else she wanted to say, but she stopped herself.

"Are you excited for the carnival, then?"

"Obviously." Grace finally seemed warmed up to him. "My dad takes me every year. We get dressed up and go all out. Always in some matching costume."

"Like what?"

"We've done Scooby-Doo and Shaggy. Thing One and Thing Two. Eggs and bacon. One year I even got him to go as the Mummy to my Dracula."

"Got anything good planned for this year?"

Grace paused then.

"I don't know." Her excitement seemed to have drained off. "I guess I'll have to go by myself this year. At least on opening night, since only students are allowed."

She looked so disappointed that Calvin couldn't help himself. He liked it when she smiled. He liked *making* her smile. It made for a prettier picture.

"We can go together. I'll be your Watson or Wolf Man or whatever you need."

"Really?"

Grace leaned forward as if she were about to wrap her arms around him. But instead, her hand fluttered to her chest, tapping something hidden underneath her shirt.

"What's that you're fiddling with?" Calvin asked.

"It's a necklace," Grace said. And then after a moment she fished it out to show him. The silver locket glimmered as Calvin leaned forward to get a better look. The charm was polished and well taken care of, its smooth edges curving into a round oval.

"What's inside?"

This seemed to make Grace nervous, but eventually she unclasped the miniature lock and opened it for him. A black-and-white photo sat nestled there, a picture of a beautiful woman with dark hair swept up and out of her face.

"Is that your mom?" Calvin asked.

But Grace didn't answer, the locket starting to shake between her fingers. She sniffled and Calvin suddenly remembered.

The car accident.

"I'm sorry. I didn't mean to—I forgot about your mom and—"

He was an insensitive idiot. And the itch—he could feel it starting, tingling in his fingers, humming in the back of his head.

"It's okay." Grace spoke softly. But at least she wasn't crying. "I miss her. But this helps me."

She held the locket up for him to get one last look, and then she slipped it back underneath her shirt.

"Do you remember that day? When we were at Elena's because of the tornado warning?"

Calvin could barely concentrate on Grace's question. His mind got lost in the slapping of volleyballs against palms and the girls' play-calling, their shouts of *line* and *angle* and *deep*. His fingers buzzed with a dire urgency.

A shrill whistle cut through the air, and Calvin couldn't take it anymore. He grabbed his notebook from the bleacher and turned to a clean page. Then, making sure to keep it angled away from Grace, he set to work, his fingers sketching on their own as he tried to stay focused on her.

"Of course," Calvin finally got out, the release almost immediate when his pen connected with paper. As the stylus started to scratch out a vision, Grace craned her neck around, but he pulled back, making sure she couldn't see.

"Well, do you remember how we went up to Elena's grandmother's room? How we played that game in the mirror?"

Calvin's pen froze, hovering just over the page.

"Did you see anyone in the mirror? When it was your turn?"

Grace's words came out slowly, her breath held for his answer.

Calvin closed his eyes and flashed back to that afternoon. The storm blowing outside. The four of them sneaking up to that bedroom, uncovering that mirror and then stepping in front of it one by one. The cursed woman he'd seen floating there in his reflection. Her taloned hand coming to rest on his shoulder. Her red lips whispering into his ear, showing him horrible things.

His eyes snapped open, and he hadn't even realized he'd started back drawing.

"No. I didn't see anything," Calvin mumbled. "Did you? I thought it was just a silly game."

He tried his best to play it off. He couldn't admit it. It sounded crazy. And he'd been nine. He couldn't trust what he thought he'd seen. What he'd imagined.

But he couldn't ignore it either. He couldn't forget the visions that followed him, the feeling of death at his back, death lying in wait. For him. For his friends. For anyone who got close.

At Grace's crestfallen face, Calvin glanced down at his sketchbook and his heart jumped into his throat. Before he even had time to process it, he lurched forward, knocking Grace off the bleachers. Her surprised yell exploded in his ears as a volleyball slammed into the stands right where she'd been sitting a second earlier.

"Are you okay?" Calvin asked, watching her carefully. Her face was flushed and her bangs stuck out in stray angles, but she looked all right. Still in one piece.

Calvin spotted his notebook lying open on the bleachers and snatched it up, closing it before Grace could see what he'd drawn. The picture of her, blood streaming from her nose, her eye swollen shut and purpling, the stray volleyball ricocheting away after beaning her, completely unsuspecting and unprepared, in the face.

"What the—"

Grace took her time sitting up, looking at where the ball had whizzed past her head. Then she turned toward the court, where all the players had stopped practice to stare up at her.

"Who hit that?" Grace's voice shook as she looked for some kind of apology.

"Don't be such a baby."

Calvin watched as Grace's back stiffened. When he looked at the court, he wasn't surprised to see the snarky retort had come out of Elena's mouth.

"Next time try watching your head. Unless you want a black eye to look like those monsters you love so much."

Elena's cackle punctuated the insult, and half the players started giggling with her. Grace froze, her arms dropping limply to her sides. Calvin thought she might start crying right there next to him. But a whistle broke the tension as Calvin's mom walked back onto the court, having missed the whole episode.

As the girls snapped into their practice formations, Calvin noticed Grace's hands clenched into fists, shaking slightly.

"Just ignore her." Calvin tried to smooth things over.

"It's fine." Grace brushed off his concern. She shrugged,

and her fingers unspooled from their balls. "I'm gonna go clean up.".

"You don't have to—" Calvin tried one last time to keep her from going, but she didn't listen.

"Thanks for the save."

And she was gone, carefully picking her way down the bleachers. When she got to the floor she hurried off, but before disappearing, she took one last moment to glare at the court, at the back of Elena's head.

CHAPTER 9
GRACE

Grace couldn't hide the skip in her step or the smile that kept appearing on her lips. She was practically floating as she made her way through the hallways, her eyes darting, searching everywhere for Calvin. She'd taken her time getting ready that morning, picking out her favorite dress—the autumn-orange one with miniature witches, black cats, broomsticks, and cauldrons sprinkled all over it. And she'd even broken out her silver jack-o'-lantern earrings. The ones she only wore on super special occasions. But this definitely qualified. It was finally happening. Her soulmate fantasy was coming true, and she wasn't going to let it slip away.

Grace got to her locker and threw her books inside, daydreaming all the while. They'd actually hung out the day before. Her and Calvin. He'd noticed her. Had called her out of a crowd. She'd been so shocked that she'd had to pinch herself to make sure she wasn't imagining it.

And then when they talked, he hadn't made fun of her. He hadn't called her a ghoul or a freak. He'd liked her movie, her T-shirts. He'd even volunteered to go with her to the opening night of the Harvest Halloween Carnival.

That was like a date. An actual date with the boy Grace had been crushing on for five years. She swooned and had to grab on to the edges of her locker to keep herself upright. Because that wasn't all.

He'd saved her. He'd knocked her out of harm's way when that volleyball had come flying right at her face. She didn't know how he'd seen it coming, but he'd stuck his neck out for her. That had to mean something. Even if Elena had tried to ruin it.

Grace leaned back and glared down the hallway. She could just make out Elena standing at her own locker, applying a fresh layer of lip gloss.

Elena with her perfect, popular life. Her adoring best friends. Her gorgeous boyfriend. And as if that weren't enough, she had some shirtless dude on standby. Right under Henry's nose. Grace stuck her head back in her locker, afraid steam might come pouring out of her ears.

But what did she care about Elena anymore? Grace had Calvin.

She flipped open her notebook and stared at Calvin's picture there. The drawing of the demon she'd found. She still hadn't asked him about it, but she would next time she saw him. Maybe it could even be a Halloween costume. He could go as the Wolf Man and she could go as his own creation. Wouldn't that be romantic? They'd for sure win best couples costume.

Picking out her books for English, Grace shut her locker and started down the hall, heading past where Elena was still primping for her next class. But right as she was about to pass Elena, someone slid in front of her and cut her off.

Grace lurched back and narrowly missed running into him. Her curiosity piqued as she recognized the boy's dark hair and sloped shoulders. As she noticed his shaking fists, the angry tilt of his chin.

Henry. But what had happened to him?

"How could you?" Henry's question seethed through his clenched jaw as Elena looked at him dumbly.

"How could I what?"

"Don't lie to me." His fist slammed into the lockers, the bang of a firecracker. Everyone who hadn't noticed the fight brewing turned to watch, a semicircle forming around the couple as their relationship took its last breaths.

"Three years and this is how—"

"Henry, I don't know what you're talking about." Elena's shout carried down the hallway and she looked to have the upper hand. But then Henry whipped out his phone and started reading.

"Are you ever going to tell me who you are? The flowers were beautiful, but when can I meet you?"

Elena gaped, her cheeks turning bright red as Henry continued to read.

"I keep imagining what it'd be like to kiss you."

"Those are private," Elena shouted desperately as she lunged forward and snatched at the phone. "How'd you even get them? Were you going through my messages?"

"Please," Henry spat. "I trusted you. I thought we'd be together forever. Which I guess makes me an idiot."

His voice broke then, and a sob hiccuped out of him. Grace's heart ached in her chest. She could barely breathe herself and didn't know how he could keep going. But Elena didn't leave any time for sympathy as she launched into her own interrogation, unmoved by his tears.

"Then how'd you get these?"

"Someone sent them to me last night." Henry had lost all his fight. Admitted defeat. "I didn't think they were real. Not at first."

"Henry." Elena tried to pull him back. "This doesn't have to be it."

Henry shrugged her off, though, giving her his saddest grimace. "Yes, it does. You don't get to do whatever you want. You don't get to toy with me and then act like it's no big deal."

"Come on. We can work this out. This—it was nothing.

78

We're meant to be, Henry. You can't deny it. It can't just be over like that. You can't just walk away from me."

But apparently Henry could. And he did, turning his back on a suddenly desperate Elena and wading through the crowd of stunned onlookers.

"You'll regret leaving me," Elena called after her now ex-boyfriend.

And then, when he didn't turn back, she slammed her palm against her locker, screaming out loud before barreling through the crowd in the opposite direction. She looked ready to feast on anyone who got in her way. She looked just like a demon, Grace thought, as she watched the girl go.

CHAPTER 10
ELENA

Rage coursed through her veins, consuming her, burning every inch of her body. Her hair could have been on fire, her eyebrows singed clean off as she stalked up the driveway and through her front door. She was so mad she didn't even feel the soreness in her feet, the tiredness from her two-mile walk home. She'd faked sick to get out of volleyball practice but hadn't wanted to call her mom. She hadn't felt like letting anyone else see her so upset. So embarrassed. So completely dumped.

Henry had broken up with *her*.

She stomped into the kitchen and slammed her keys down on the counter. No one was home, so she could let her tantrum fly.

She still couldn't believe it. Didn't Henry know how good he had it? Didn't he realize she was the best thing going in his life? Everyone was jealous of him. Everyone wanted to be him because he was with *her*. So what if she'd been texting another guy? Was Henry saying that she shouldn't talk to anyone ever? Was he really that controlling?

He doesn't deserve you.

Elena turned as the whisper slipped into her ear. But it was only the dish cabinet behind her, the wineglasses glinting in the light, her reflection barely visible in each one.

You're so much better than him. So much better without him.

The thought echoed through her head, each of her reflections taking its turn to speak.

And weren't they right? He'd only ever dragged her down. She was in high school. She should be making her mark— hanging out with upperclassmen, getting invited to their parties, going on dates with them. Kissing them.

Henry was her *middle school* boyfriend. He was immature, a kid. He couldn't keep up with her. He was holding her back and even he knew it.

He wanted to knock you down. He wanted to mortify you.

The fire in Elena sparked and spat. It grew teeth and then bared them. Because it was true. Henry hadn't just dumped her. He'd embarrassed her. And he'd chosen to do it in front of everybody. Right in the middle of the hallway. In the middle of the school day. He'd wanted her to look like the bad guy, like a cheater.

He wanted you to lose.

Elena looked up suddenly and was caught off guard by

her full-length reflection staring back at her—her eyes red with rage, her hands balled into fists at her sides. She startled back, hardly recognizing herself. And then she realized where she was.

When had she left the kitchen? And why had she come up here? Into her grandmother's old bedroom?

She glanced around, and a tingle crawled up her spine. With the shades drawn, the room was eerily dark. But the mirror—it was like someone had thrown a spotlight on it. Its glass shined white like the full moon. And the curlicue script running all around it glittered brilliantly. Elena took a few hesitant steps forward, her reflection in the center of the mirror glowing, cool and radiant, her red eyes and clenched fists gone.

Look at you. So young. So beautiful. You don't deserve this.
She didn't.
So what are you going to do about it?

Elena watched as her jaw clenched, her lips pressing into a determined grimace. She was going to get even. She was going to embarrass Henry. She was going to ruin him just like he'd tried to ruin her. She was going to make him regret that he ever broke up with her. And she was going to enjoy every second of it.

He's not the only one who wronged you.

She gasped, her anger exploding when the fresh oxygen hit her lungs. How could she not have realized it until now? Her text messages hadn't just magically appeared on Henry's phone. Someone had sent them.

But who? No one knew about her anonymous admirer. She hadn't told a single one of her girlfriends. And even if someone had found out, they wouldn't have been able to grab her phone. Not without her seeing.

You know who.

Elena's gaze snapped back up to her reflection, getting lost in her own eyes as she thought. And then, suddenly, it came to her. Someone had seen her messages. And that person had access to her phone. To her gym locker.

Steph.

The name scorched through every muscle in Elena's body. It all made sense. Steph hated her. She wanted to be her. She was jealous that Coach Lee had named them co-captains. She would do anything to take that spot for herself.

The thoughts jumbled in Elena's mind, spreading like wildfire.

Steph is a liar. Steph wants to ruin you. Steph is the enemy.

Her anger—it burned so hot. So brightly. It pulsed through her, spreading out of her control. Elena screamed and her fist flew forward. Connected with the glass.

A sharp crack filled the air as Elena pulled her trembling fist back. Shards of glass fell to the floor and a drop of blood dripped from her knuckles.

She gaped at the broken glass, the mirror that was now

missing a chunk. A network of cracks spiderwebbed out across the whole surface of it, her reflection broken into a hundred disjointed pieces.

What had she done?

Fear squeezed Elena's lungs so that she could barely breathe. She was going to get in so much trouble when her parents found out—

But they wouldn't. Not unless she told them. No one ever came in here. She just had to hide the evidence.

Elena scurried to pick up the bigger shards of glass that had fallen on the floor. Then, after throwing them into a garbage bag that she'd take out to the dumpster later, she picked up the white sheet that had been covering the mirror. She held the fabric tightly between her fingers and snapped it, watching the dust billow out like a cloud of smoke. She snapped it again and again before throwing the sheet over the mirror and covering up the damage.

As she hurried out of the bedroom, Elena took one last look over her shoulder, her eyes sweeping the floor, making sure she hadn't missed any large pieces of glass. Satisfied, she closed the door behind her, leaving before she could notice the sheet move. A clawed hand thrust forward, grasping for a way out.

CHAPTER 11
STEPH

She'd dreamed about her again last night.

That dark swoop of short hair. That cute nose scrunched in concentration, eyes turned up in thought. The tip of a pencil tap, tap, tapping against the blank page. Tapping and then finally writing, the words a steady stream of short strokes. They were bold, yet indecipherable no matter how hard Steph squinted, no matter how close she tried to get. She could only watch the girl write and imagine what worlds the words were creating as they filled the page.

Maybe one where the two of them actually found each other. Maybe one where they could be together.

A locker clanged next to Steph and she jolted forward, nearly banging her head. She looked down at the books in her hands and realized she'd grabbed the wrong ones. What had gotten into her?

Steph sighed. She'd been stuck in this daze all morning. She'd dreamed about the girl from the mirror before, but last night had felt different. It'd felt like a premonition. Like the girl had been real. Like she was waiting for Steph to find her.

But why would today be any different than the last five years? And hadn't she already decided that *this* wasn't something she could let herself be? Not now, at least. And maybe not ever.

Still, Steph couldn't help but hold on to the hope that something miraculous could happen. That there was someone out there waiting for her, someone who'd accept her, Bigfoot frame and all. Someone who'd find her beautiful.

A soulmate.

"Sasquatch!"

Steph jerked back as her locker door slammed shut in front of her face, nearly taking her nose off. Shell-shocked, she turned and found Elena, a head shorter, glaring up at her.

"We need to talk," Elena said, her voice clipped and to the point.

Steph rolled her eyes and relaxed a bit. "And how have I offended you today?"

Elena she could deal with. She'd dealt with her all year. But Steph did find it odd that she hadn't brought her friends along as backup.

"You know what you did." Elena shot forward, standing on her tiptoes to get right in Steph's face. Steph could feel Elena's breath on her cheek, her nostrils streaming steam.

"Look," Steph sighed, fed up with having this argument. "I don't want to co-captain with you either. But Coach made the call. And now we have to work together. Unless you plan on quitting."

Elena shuddered back as if Steph had smacked her across the face. "You'd like that, wouldn't you?"

"Honestly?" Steph could hear the exasperation in her own voice. "I'd like to quit having this fight. I'd like us to just get along. Or at least agree to leave each other alone."

Elena laughed—one short, humorless sound, like a balloon popping.

"It's too late for that," Elena whispered, her words a threat.

And something in Steph stirred.

Usually she would have ignored Elena, let the girl think she'd won. But a boldness leapt into her throat. Why should she back down? What was it she was so afraid of? What did she have to lose by fighting back?

"Look, I don't know what your problem is." Steph's voice held firm, didn't quiver one bit. "But you need to get over it. I've tried being nice to you. I've tried ignoring your insults. But I'm sick of it. I'm not playing along with your games anymore. I'm done."

"My games?" Elena spat back. "You know what my problem is with you? It's that you're trying to ruin my life. You're trying to make me look bad in front of Coach. Trying to take my team away from me. And now you're trying to break up me and Henry."

Steph's brow furrowed in confusion, but Elena plowed on, running over any words Steph might have thrown back at her.

"It's not going to work. I'm onto you. I know what you did, and I'm not going to let you win. I won't lose. Not to you!"

Elena banged her fist against Steph's locker, the sound echoing like a gunshot through the hallway. And then, before Steph could get out another word, before she could even try to make sense of all the accusations that had just been thrown at her, Elena stalked away.

But Steph wasn't going to let her have it. Not this time.

That same boldness churned in her gut. Anger mixed with courage, and her adrenaline spiked. She wheeled around and took off after Elena, weaving between classmates, her long legs making up ground quickly. She reached out, ready to yank Elena back by the shoulder—by her hair if she had to—and then she froze.

Her rage left her. It evaporated right there on the spot.

Wonder took its place, disbelief emptying her mind. She stared across the hallway, blinking, sure her eyes were playing tricks on her, sure her dreams were spilling over.

Because it was her. The girl from the mirror. In the flesh. Pencil tucked behind one ear. Backpack hanging off one shoulder. Her face scrunched up, studying the piece of paper in her hands.

It was really her.

CHAPTER 12
CALVIN

A sharp ache throbbed at the back of Calvin's head. He tried to rub it away, but he knew it was already too late. The migraine would take hold in no time. Unless he gave in.

But it was too soon for that. It'd only been an hour since his last sketch, when he'd drawn Vice Principal Matthis skidding in the hallway, careening down the stairwell and landing in a pile on the floor, his foot bent at an unnatural angle.

And then the vice principal had actually slipped. Luckily, he'd only fallen one step down before catching himself. He'd only twisted his ankle. But still—

Calvin's drawings, as disturbing as they were, had never come true. Grace had been a close call in the gym the other day, but no one had ever actually gotten hurt. And his visions had never gotten this bad this quickly. They'd never felt so insistent. It was like someone had his head in a nutcracker, squeezing harder little by little until his skull might burst.

Calvin squirmed in his seat. He tried to focus on his teacher and follow along with the lesson, anything to keep his mind busy. He picked up his pencil to take notes but then quickly dropped it.

He couldn't trust himself. Not with lead or ink. An errant doodle and the images would come pouring out. They'd reveal disaster. A tragedy that would only be more horrible because now, he was afraid it might actually come true.

Above the board, the clock ticked, and Calvin latched onto that. He counted along, passing thirty and then sixty. At 120, he thought he could do it. At 180, he started to sweat. As he hit 300 and 360, he couldn't help but grimace. His whole body felt tight, every muscle clenched. His fingers twisted into gnarled knots, waiting for the doomsday clock to tick down.

He was going to go crazy. His eyes were going to pop out of his skull and roll across his desk like squishy marbles. They'd fall unseen to the floor, where someone would unknowingly crush them underfoot.

And wouldn't that be a relief? A release from this torture?

The pressure in his head built, a volcano primed to erupt, and Calvin couldn't take it anymore. His eyes shut and the images rushed in at him.

Flashes of disaster. Of car wrecks and runaway trains. Of roller coaster crashes. Of drownings and house fires and tornadoes. Of an E. coli outbreak. Of hospital wards filled to capacity, patients young and old hooked up to oxygen tubes. Of screaming matches and divorced parents. Of being cold and hungry and all alone. Of fear.

It flooded through Calvin, each vision taking a piece of him with it, hollowing him out until he had nothing left. Nothing except the pain.

His eyes flew open then, a cold sweat dousing his forehead. He watched as a stray droplet slid down the lens of his glasses. He blinked and looked up at the board, but it didn't seem like anyone had noticed.

Had he fallen asleep?

He squinted at the clock, but only a few minutes had passed.

He'd never blacked out like that. What had just happened?

A grogginess clogged Calvin's thoughts. The sharp ache burrowing through his skull had disappeared, but he didn't exactly feel better. Something else had taken its place—an emptiness, cold and clinging. It weighed him down, his arms and legs and head almost too heavy to lift.

A knock came at the classroom door and Calvin's teacher paused the lesson. As he capped his dry-erase marker to check on the interruption, Calvin flexed his fingers out of habit. But something wasn't right. He let his gaze dip to the desk, to the pen sitting firmly between his fingers.

His hand shook and the pen came loose. He didn't recall picking it up, or opening his notebook, for that matter. But looking at the flurry of fresh pages in front of him, he knew that he must have.

Only—the pages were still blank. Or mostly blank. They were empty except for the upper-right-hand corner. Calvin slid his fingers under the open sheet of paper and lifted it closer so he could inspect the drawing.

It was the demon. *His* demon. The thing that had haunted him for the past five years. Dark lips and bloody tears dotting its cheeks. He flipped the page and realized that he'd drawn another one, identical to the first. And another underneath that. And again underneath that.

Calvin paged back and the drawings kept coming. But now he noticed that the demon was changing in tiny ways. Its hair and nose. The blood on its face. He suddenly understood what he'd done.

He turned back to the first picture, took the corners of the pages in his hand, and flipped through them quickly, watching as the demon transformed in front of his eyes. It lost its cruel edge, growing softer and prettier as it became a completely different person.

"Everyone." Calvin's teacher's voice carried through the room, and Calvin reluctantly pulled his eyes away from his notebook. "We have a new student joining us today."

And as Calvin's eyes swept over the girl standing in the front of the room, his breath seized in his chest. His fingers curled around the edge of his desk, the only things keeping him from falling out of his seat. He gawked at the new girl, his thoughts suddenly blank. Because it didn't make sense. It was impossible.

His eyes flicked from her face to his drawing. He flipped through the pages of his notebook again and again and again, watching the demon morph. Watching its hair grow shorter, its face smooth out, its eyes twinkle brighter. Watching the pencil stub appear behind its right ear. Watching as the demon became the very person standing in front of him now. This flesh-and-blood girl.

CHAPTER 13
STEPH

"Our fearless co-captain has finally arrived," Elena announced as Steph followed her into the living room where the rest of the team had set up for the night.

Steph swallowed her grimace. She didn't point out that Elena had purposely sent her the wrong time for the sleepover. That she'd had her show up two hours late as some sort of prank. Was she trying to humiliate her? Or make her look like an idiot? Did Elena really think that something so stupid would make Steph quit the team?

Steph wouldn't be broken so easily.

"I hope you all saved a face mask for me," she replied, pasting on her best smile, her hands clenched around her gym bag like they were wrapped around Elena's throat. But she had to be on her best behavior tonight. She had to win these girls over. So she ignored Elena's fake cheer and waded in.

It was like a bomb had exploded in there—a pink, glitter-filled, sugary-sweet, nail-polish-and-hair-curler kind of weapon. Colorful beads and ribbons and thread were piled on the coffee table, and there were bowls of popcorn and candy scattered throughout the room. There was even a platter of cupcakes, which it looked like the girls had iced earlier in the night.

And the girls—her teammates—she'd never seen them so animated, so at ease. They looked like sisters. Like they'd known one another for years, chattering away, laughing their heads off, wearing pajamas and looking completely comfortable as they gave one another manicures and made friendship brace-lets and fought over the last kernels of popcorn.

Was this what sleepovers were supposed to be like? Spending the night at her aunt Ellen's house with her younger brother hadn't exactly prepared her.

"You're here." Kayleigh, their middle hitter, leapt to her feet and wrapped Steph in an instant hug. "I was worried you were sick or something."

"Just running a little late," Steph assured her and the rest of the girls, trying not to appear uncomfortable with all those eyes suddenly turned on her.

"Come and help me finish my hair."

And Steph followed, watching the back of Kayleigh's head, marveling at the half of her hair that was already twisted into an intricate design that ran behind her ear and down her neck.

"I don't know how to do that," Steph admitted as she dropped her bag and sat down on the floor.

"It's easy," Julia, their libero, said as she leaned over, her long red hair already swept into a plaited crown that ringed the top of her head. Her fingers moved slowly as she showed Steph the pattern, finishing the braid and then undoing her hard work.

"Now, you try."

"I don't know," Steph began nervously.

"If you mess up, I can always fix it."

Steph couldn't argue with that, so she picked up Kayleigh's hair and did her best.

"Not bad," Julia said, examining Steph's work. And it actually wasn't terrible. But it wasn't great either, a feeling Julia confirmed as her fingers moved lightning quick and rewove Kayleigh's hair into a perfectly tight plait.

"You'll have it down in no time," Kayleigh assured Steph as she inspected her hair with the camera on her phone. "Here, get in the pic."

And Kayleigh's arm reached out and pulled Steph over, squashing their heads together as she grinned at the camera.

"So cute," Kayleigh exclaimed as she showed Steph and then started typing, reading her caption out loud. *Team bonding has never looked this good #volleyballislife.*

Steph blushed as a strange feeling swirled in her stomach. She'd never had girlfriends. Not like this. But maybe the team could be like a second family. She'd always wondered what it'd be like to have sisters.

"Oh my god, Kayleigh," Elena gushed suddenly from across the room. "James is not going to be able to resist you. It's so fab."

"Speaking of boys," Julia drawled out. "Whatever happened with you and Henry?"

Elena's smile faded, but she rebounded a millisecond later.

"We decided to go our separate ways," Elena replied, picking through a box of nail polish as if her breakup were no big deal. "I mean, we're in high school now. Time to grow up. We both thought it'd be good to try seeing other people."

Steph swallowed down the words that had leapt into her throat. She'd seen Elena and Henry's breakup—as had half of the freshman class—and there was nothing mutual about it. But she didn't want to blow up Elena's spot. It wouldn't get Steph or the team anywhere. They still needed to come together.

"How about you, Steph?" Elena asked, her tone sweet and innocent. "Got your eyes on anyone?"

"No," Steph sputtered, her face flushing an embarrassing red.

"What about Coach Lee's son?" Kayleigh asked.

"Oh, Calvin's cute," Julia piped up encouragingly.

"I mean . . ." Elena drew the words out, making sure everyone was listening. "He wouldn't be my first choice. But you do you, Steph."

"No, I don't—" Steph struggled to get the words out. "I don't have a thing for Calvin."

"He is a bit of a weirdo." Elena spoke like she was agreeing with something Steph had said. "Really quiet. And what is he always drawing in that notebook? Very creepy."

"I didn't say—" Steph tried to clarify. Because she did like Calvin. He'd always been nice to her during their carpool days, at least. She just didn't like him in that way.

You don't like any boys in that way.

Steph yelped as the thought popped into her head. Her eyes shot up and darted around the room, afraid someone else might have heard.

"It's okay if you like Calvin," Elena teased, drawing Steph's attention again as she chose a color and started working on her nails. "We won't judge you. I mean, it's not like you've got a crush on one of *us*. Now *that'd* be weird."

And if Steph hadn't been watching Elena's lips moving when the words had come out, she might have imagined it was all in her head.

Because it was her absolute nightmare. And the reason she couldn't be—wasn't gay. The girls would never trust her. They'd act weird around her, afraid she might be checking them out. It'd only give them another reason to shun her.

Luckily, Steph was saved as the doorbell rang and Elena's mom came into the room to announce that pizza had arrived. The girls all clambered to their feet and hustled for the kitchen, Elena's comment forgotten by everyone.

But not by Steph.

Better not let them see who you really are.

And she wouldn't. Her gaze darted to Elena and then back down. She'd hold on to her secret for as long as she could. Even if that meant she had to take a back seat to Elena. At least for tonight.

"Steph." Elena had found her again, calling over the kitchen island. "You're not even in your pajamas yet."

Steph glanced down at her sweatpants and T-shirt. She hadn't even noticed all the other girls were in tank tops and brightly colored pajama pants.

"You brought some, didn't you?"

Steph didn't know what to say.

"You can borrow a pair of mine," Elena insisted. "You'll be way comfier."

And though Steph was perfectly happy in the clothes she had on, she knew she couldn't refuse the offer. But she'd keep her eyes open. She wouldn't let Elena trick her again.

"Here, I'll grab them from my room. And I can show you where you're sleeping while we're upstairs."

Steph nodded again, swallowing her last bite of pizza, and followed Elena out of the kitchen.

"It's really going well, don't you think?" Elena chattered innocently enough. "Everyone's bonding and getting along. Starting to trust each other."

"Yeah. The sleepover was a great idea. Thanks for organizing and hosting it and all."

Steph held back as Elena dug through her drawers. "Don't mention it. It's nothing a good captain wouldn't do."

And Steph had to make a conscious effort not to throw the *co-* in Elena's face. And not to toss back the pair of hot-pink pajama pants Elena handed her.

"You're gonna be sleeping down the hall," Elena explained, pushing Steph out of her doorway. "Unfortunately, my room's all full."

If Elena had expected Steph to be upset by this announcement, she would be disappointed. Steph was perfectly happy to sleep in a different room from her conniving co-captain. That way she wouldn't wake up with peanut butter on her face or her clothes frozen into a solid block of ice.

"No worries. I know there are a lot of us."

"You'll be in here."

Elena had stopped at the end of the hall. And Steph remembered the bedroom the second she stepped foot inside. She recognized the furniture and bedspread. The keepsakes sitting on top of the dresser. She'd been here before. Five years ago.

"Wasn't this your grandmother's room?"

Elena gave her a puzzled look, but then seemed to remember. "That's right. I'd forgotten we used to carpool."

An awkward beat passed between them.

"Well, just be careful. And try not to break anything."

Steph noticed Elena glancing nervously at the shrouded mirror as she said this.

"You can get changed and then meet us back downstairs. I think it's time for a round of Truth or Dare."

Steph nodded and tried to look excited, even though the game could only get her in trouble. Then with a flounce, Elena disappeared.

Alone finally, Steph let herself exhale. She stretched her neck to both sides and winced as her bones cracked. She hadn't realized how tense she'd been. How wound up she got around Elena, worried about every word out of her mouth and what it might reveal. It was so much easier on the court. Her play could do the talking.

She moved over to the bed and set her bag down. But glancing around the room, she noticed that hers was the only duffel there. Elena wouldn't have stuck her in here by herself, would she? Steph weighed the hot-pink pajama pants as she thought.

Actually, it sounded like exactly the kind of thing Elena would do. Isolate the competition.

She let the pajamas slip through her fingers and fall onto the bed. She needed a minute. Or maybe five. She pushed her hands back through her hair and pulled the strands into a ponytail. Her legs hummed and she started pacing around the small room, feeling suddenly restless.

Did Elena know? Did she suspect? Was that why she'd thrown her in this room all by herself?

Steph's doubts hurtled by, moving faster than she could walk. Faster than she could think.

Was that Elena's plan to get the captain spot all to herself?

Steph froze as the thought hit her.

Then the closet door groaned, and Steph caught the glimpse of a shadow dancing across the wall. She jumped, her heart in her throat, and turned, expecting to find one of the other girls there, her roommate for the night. But she was alone.

She knew she'd heard something, though. She wasn't imagining it. She took a few steps toward the closet and squinted as she peered into its dark belly, her scalp prickling, waiting for something to jump out at her.

When nothing did, she pulled back, pushing the closet door the rest of the way shut. She glanced back at the wall, tracing the shadow's path, remembering how it had dipped low before disappearing. Before it had hidden away.

She took a few cautious steps and found herself standing in front of the shrouded mirror. The one that they'd played their game in all those years ago.

It had seemed childish back then. But now—now Steph had seen that girl in the halls at school. Did that mean that it was real? Was she Steph's soulmate?

Steph hadn't worked up the courage to talk to her. She was too afraid, terrified that it'd confirm the truth. That Steph liked girls. That she was gay.

But that hadn't stopped her from looking for the girl, marveling over the way her stomach fluttered and her heart thumped faster every time she caught glimpses of her in the halls.

Admit it. You're in love.

Steph startled and she realized she'd moved closer to the mirror. What would happen if she took another peek? Would she see the girl again? It couldn't hurt, could it?

Her hand hovered in front of her, reaching for the sheet, ready to pull it aside.

"Boo!"

Steph screamed as the shadow reappeared suddenly, lunging at her from behind the mirror, its sharp fingers set to rake her open, to spill blood all over the floor. She shot backward, her legs knocking into the edge of the bed. Her arms windmilled in giant circles as she tried to catch her balance, but she couldn't hold on and flopped unceremoniously onto her back, the mattress groaning underneath her sudden weight.

It was then that Steph heard a familiar cackle at the bedroom door. She turned and saw Elena smiling wickedly down at her, the girl's phone out and recording. Over by the mirror, Kayleigh moved into view, laughing her head off, too. And Steph, her face reddening with embarrassment, realized that Elena had set up this whole embarrassing episode.

"You should have seen your face," Elena said around her smirk. "Oh wait, you can."

And she flipped her phone around so Steph could watch the whole thing. Kayleigh leaping out from behind the mirror to scare her. Steph's tall frame falling back onto the bed like a clumsy, oversized oaf. Like the giant crashing down from its beanstalk.

"Timber."

Then right there in front of Steph's eyes, Elena attached the video to a text message and sent it out to their entire team.

She was enjoying this too much, rewatching the clip over and over again as Kayleigh joined her at the bedroom door.

"See you downstairs," Elena quipped, and then the girls disappeared, their laughter echoing down the hallway, ringing in Steph's ears as she wallowed in her embarrassment.

She wanted to curl up in the comforter and not show her face for the rest of the night. She wanted to disappear. She wanted to crack Elena's head open, watch it deflate like a punctured volleyball.

Steph jolted up off the bed, fear coursing through her. Where had that rage come from? It scared her that she could think such terrible thoughts. That she could imagine her fist smashing right through Elena's skull.

But she couldn't let Elena ruin the night. She couldn't let her win.

She got to her feet and picked up the pajama pants. Hot pink wasn't really her color, but she didn't have any other option. She changed quickly and tucked her old clothes into her duffel bag. Then she bent over and hid her stuff under the bed. Better not to give Elena the chance at another easy prank.

As she straightened back up, Steph's eyes fell on the covered mirror. She thought about their game again. About the girl she'd seen in its depths. She closed her eyes and that face flashed in front of her. The same girl she'd spotted in the hallway earlier that week. But could it really be?

She studied that face in her mind's eye, relishing every detail. The spritely nose and inquisitive eyes. That short, smooth hair that she longed to run her fingers through.

Lightning flickered across the memory and the face shifted in a flash. The girl grew fangs. The corners of her mouth dripped blood. Her hair curled into long reptilian coils. A stench crept up Steph's nose. Like rotted flowers. Sickly sweet and foul. Roses left out on a gravestone for months.

Steph's eyes shot open. They frantically searched the room, but she was all alone. No one hiding in wait to scare her out of her pajama pants.

What was she even doing thinking like that? Thinking about soulmates? She didn't have time for romance. Especially not one with a girl. She couldn't afford to let her guard down. She couldn't give Elena any more openings. She had a team to win over. A sleepover to get back to.

CHAPTER 14
GRACE

It was one of those perfect autumn days, the leaves half-turned to brilliant reds and oranges, a comfortable chill running underneath the air, summer's last breath going out. It was the kind of day Grace lived for, when she got to impersonate her favorite mystery-solving cartoon and break out her chunkiest sweater—the pumpkin-orange one with the thick collar that came all the way up to her chin. And since it was spirit week at school, they even got to eat lunch out on the front lawn. They got to enjoy the weather before it got too cold.

Grace's lunch box squeaked as she opened the lid and pulled out her sandwich. She took a bite and raspberry jam spilled from the corners of her mouth.

"You've got something there," Calvin said, dropping his pen and pointing as he tried not to laugh.

Grace slapped her hand over her lips, sure she looked like

some kind of vampire. She wiped her face clean and then carefully took another bite, nibbling at the sandwich now, ignoring her grumbling stomach.

"What are you drawing?"

Calvin had picked up his pen and started scratching at his notebook again. Grace tried to sneak a glance, but he was good at covering it up.

"Just sketching," Calvin replied casually, his eyes flitting up from the page to meet Grace's even though his pen kept moving.

"You're always sketching. But you've never shown me any of your drawings."

Calvin's hand stilled, his eyes locked on Grace's. An awkward moment passed between them.

"Sure I have," Calvin finally replied, staring back down at his work, edging the notebook a little farther away. "My Wolf Man T-shirt. That's a Calvin Lee original."

Grace nodded, remembering. But he was always drawing in that notebook of his. He had to have more than just the one finished picture. Hadn't he ever entered a contest? Or had to present a project for art class?

Then Grace remembered that she still had the sketch she'd picked up on the stairwell—the demon in all its grim glory. She glanced at her own stack of notebooks and pulled over the binder on top. She flipped it open and took out the folded-up piece of paper.

"This is yours, too, right?"

Calvin's eyes bugged out and his pen thumped against his notebook. Carefully, he reached over and took it from her, his hands trembling slightly.

"Where'd you get this?"

"I found it a couple of weeks ago. On the stairwell where you'd been drawing. I assumed it was yours."

Should she not have mentioned it? It was just a drawing, after all.

"I mean, I think it's really cool. Is she like a banshee or harpy or—"

"She's a succubus."

The way Calvin murmured it, like he was legitimately afraid, only made Grace more intrigued.

"She preys on the weak, the defenseless, those who don't even know that she's there."

"She sounds scary."

Grace had leaned in close, a thrill running through her.

"Here, you can keep it." Calvin shoved the page back at Grace like it might burn his hands if he held on to it.

"But be careful," he warned, his voice a whisper. "She's dangerous."

Grace didn't know what to say as Calvin's head dipped down and he got back to his latest sketch. So she stared at the picture instead, the demon's ferocity terrifying on the page, blood on its lips and murder in its eyes. She could see why this creature would be dangerous.

But only in the movies. Or in a fairy tale.

The monster couldn't do any true harm, Grace assured herself. Not out here in the real world. Then she folded the picture up and tucked it back into the front pocket of her binder.

She regretted bringing it out. It was creepy that she'd found it, held on to it. There was an uncomfortable tension between them now and she didn't know what to say. Calvin wouldn't even look up at her, so her eyes wandered across the lawn instead.

She spotted Steph first, leaning her back against a tree, her head tilted up to the sky, lost in whatever clouds she was seeing up there. And then there was Elena, not too far away, sitting on a picnic blanket surrounded by a group of her friends.

But then Elena leapt to her feet, taking quick, decisive steps across the lawn. Grace narrowed her eyes and realized she was heading straight for Henry. Henry, who was looking pretty comfortable sitting next to one of the girls from the volleyball team. The redhead, Julia.

"What's your favorite candy?"

Grace blinked, surprised by the question as she focused back in on Calvin. "My what?"

She watched as Calvin reached into his bag and pulled out a handful of fun-sized candy bars.

"I raided my mom's Halloween stash."

Grace's eyes lit up. Because trick-or-treating candy was just another one of the things that made Halloween her favorite holiday. When she was little she'd always hoarded her candy, hiding it from her mom and dad, making sure to ration it out so that it would last until Christmas, when she could replenish her stores with stocking candy.

"Twix are my favorite," Grace said, her hand darting to pick one out of the pile. "But I also love a Milky Way."

She grabbed one of those, too, but kept herself from eating it.

"I go for anything that has crunch or caramel," Calvin said as he picked out a rectangle of chocolate and stuffed it in his mouth. Grace followed suit and took a bite of the mini Twix.

As she chewed, she couldn't believe how well things were going between them. It was almost like they *were* soulmates. Like they *were* meant to be. Maybe what she'd seen in that mirror had been real and not just her imagination messing with her.

Grace swallowed and looked over at him, the sun shining off his dark hair, his eyebrows furrowed as he concentrated on his drawing, his glasses slipping to the end of his nose. Had he ever been cuter?

She should tell him.

What if he doesn't like you back?

Grace froze as doubt slipped in.

What if he rejects you?

She couldn't let the fear win out.

What if he hurts you?

And with that thought, Grace felt a pair of hands press down on her shoulders. A frozen breath brushed against her ear. Nails dug into her neck as the phantom fingers squeezed tighter, her throat closing up. It was a feeling she'd been familiar with over the years, but she'd never felt it this intensely before. It scared her.

But Calvin would never hurt her. He was sweet. He'd been nothing but nice to her.

Grace managed to shake off the bad feeling. She felt the claws retract and fly away ahead of her, moving on to their next victim.

She had to tell Calvin how she felt. She had to tell him now, before she lost the courage. But as Grace opened her mouth to say it, multiple things happened all at once, everything slowing down around her so that she could take it all in.

First, Calvin jumped to his feet, his notebook falling to the ground, lying there open on the grass as panic contorted his face into something scary and unrecognizable, a shout welling up in his throat.

At the same time, a loud yelp drew Grace's attention away from the boy. And as she swiveled her head to the side, she spotted Steph, a look of shock evident on her face as she struggled to get to her feet.

And then there was a piercing scream. The shriek of tires. The thud of metal denting in on itself. Glass crunching. A body thrown up and then hammered down to the ground.

Grace's hands flew to her mouth as she watched the violence of it. As she recognized the body slumped in a pile of motionless limbs on the pavement, the car he had just been hit by screeching to a halt a few feet away.

Henry.

And Elena standing there on the curb, her hands thrown up, a splatter of red dotting her cheeks, her mouth open wide, silent after her scream had shredded her throat.

The world suddenly careened back to its normal speed, giving Grace whiplash. Her whole body shook. Tears leaked from the corners of her eyes. She couldn't believe it. She'd never seen something so horrible. She wanted to rush over, to help out in any way she could. But her feet wouldn't budge. She glanced down at her boots, expecting to see herself frozen to the spot. But there was no ice gripping her toes. Only Calvin's notebook.

Grace squinted, her eyes quickly taking in the drawing but unable to process what she was seeing. It didn't make sense. It wasn't possible. Still shaking, she bent over and picked it up, bringing it right to her nose so she could examine it more closely.

The ink shimmered on the page, fresh from Calvin's pen.

"I swear, it's not what it looks like." Calvin's voice trembled, pulling Grace's attention away from the picture and back to the disaster in front of them.

"But how could you have known?" Grace tapped the notebook, not believing the proof in front of her eyes. "How could you have drawn this before it even happened?"

"I—"

But Calvin's reply was cut short as Vice Principal Matthis flung open the front doors of the school and came racing out onto the lawn. He had a walkie-talkie pressed close to his lips, shouting orders into it so quickly that Grace couldn't understand any of them.

But that didn't matter right now. And neither did Calvin's picture or what would have possessed him to draw it in the first place.

What mattered was Henry. Getting him help. Making sure he was still alive. So Grace pulled herself away from Calvin and hurried after their vice principal, cutting through the small crowd of students craning to get a better look.

He had to be okay. He couldn't be dead. She couldn't have just watched someone—

Grace broke through to the front of the group of onlookers and came up short, gasping as she caught sight of Henry.

Blood and guts never fazed her in horror movies, but here in real life, seeing someone she knew bruised and bloody and broken, seeing his arm bent at an unnatural and scary angle—it was almost too much for her to stomach. She hadn't expected it to be so gruesome. She hadn't expected Henry to look so much like a corpse, unmoving and pale.

In the distance a siren wailed, but Grace worried the

ambulance might not get there in time. Henry might really be gone.

But as she stared down at him, his arm twitched. His head turned slowly to the side to look up at them, a croak escaping his lips.

Relief washed over Grace just in time for the paramedics to arrive, rushing to get Henry strapped to a gurney, off to the hospital, where the doctors could set his arm and make him better. But as they carted Henry away, Grace couldn't keep her thoughts from turning to Calvin.

How had he drawn that scene—the accident—moments before it had happened? How had he predicted the future? And what else did he have tucked away in that notebook of his? What other disasters had he seen?

CHAPTER 15
ELENA

She hadn't done it. She had a conscience, even if no one else believed her. She hadn't pushed him. She couldn't have hurt anyone like that. Especially not Henry.

Elena tried her best to hold on to that, her head cradled in her lap, her legs pulled up and curled into a tight ball against her chest. Her whole body trembled, the trauma of that moment—of that horrible accident that had come out of nowhere—playing on a loop in her head.

She hadn't done it. She didn't have that kind of cruelty in her.

But why, then, did she have to try so hard to convince herself of that? Why did she have doubts?

Elena buried her fingers in her hair, twisting the strands into a tangled nest.

Because she didn't know. Not for sure.

When she closed her eyes and thought back to that moment,

all she could see was her rage. Her apocalyptic fury at Henry. That he would be talking to another girl right there in front of her. That he'd be flirting with someone else only a few days after they'd broken up. He shouldn't have moved on so quickly. Especially not with Julia, one of her teammates.

Elena squeezed her eyes shut harder, but she still couldn't visualize exactly what had happened. She couldn't remember how Henry had stumbled off the curb and into the street. Only that they'd been fighting. That her arms had flown up in anger. That she had screamed at him, and then just as suddenly screamed *for* him.

The sounds came back to her. The sickening crunch of the hood of the car. And then the crack of the windshield splintering. The tumbling thuds as Henry rolled over the top of the car and crashed back down on the trunk and then the pavement. How his body sat there so still, a pile of jumbled limbs, his blood the only thing moving as it oozed out of the scratches on his arms and the gash across his forehead.

A shudder ran through Elena and her eyes snapped open to find three pairs staring back at her.

"What are you looking at?"

Elena knew she sounded vile, but she didn't care. She'd thought she was alone. She didn't want anyone seeing her this upset.

"You missed a spot," Grace said quietly as she leaned forward with a tissue.

Elena snatched the Kleenex and pulled out her phone, using the camera to inspect her cheeks. Her hands shook as she scrubbed away the last bit of Henry's blood. A text message popped up on her phone and she quickly tapped it away, ignoring her anonymous admirer's concerned words. She didn't have time to deal with him now. Not when Henry could have died. Not when she could have been the one who pushed him.

"Are you all right?" Grace asked eventually, swallowing the lump building in her throat.

"Of course not," Elena spat out, using the anger to cover up her fear and anxiety. She couldn't let them see any weakness.

"Things looked pretty heated between you two."

Elena's eyes flicked to the other side of the room, where Steph had her arms folded across her chest, a frown pursing her lips together.

"What are you all even doing here?"

Elena threw the question out to everyone—Steph, Grace, and Calvin—because she couldn't stomach the thought that Steph might have the upper hand on her here.

"Vice Principal Matthis asked for any eyewitnesses to come and give a statement," Steph explained coolly.

"And you all saw what happened?"

Hope flickered in Elena's chest, beating alongside her heart. Would they be able to tell her what had happened? Clear her name?

But no one spoke up. In fact, they only looked more uneasy, sharing sideways glances with one another.

"What did you see?" Elena demanded, uncertainty creeping back in. Had she done it? Had she lost control in that moment of anger?

"We saw you all fighting," Steph finally broke the silence. "And then Henry was in the street."

"But how'd he get there?" Elena demanded.

Suddenly, Steph looked uncomfortable, her earlier smugness replaced by something skittish. Usually Elena would have reveled in this power, but right now she needed answers.

"What about you two?" she asked, turning quickly to face Grace and Calvin.

"I was there, but I didn't see exactly what happened," Grace replied, picking at her fingernails and refusing to meet Elena's gaze while Calvin looked white as milk beside her, his eyes big and glassy and far away.

"If you didn't see anything, then why are you here?" Elena nearly lost it, her frustration boiling over.

A few tense moments passed before Grace mustered a quiet reply.

"Because of this."

And she motioned to Calvin. But he refused to budge, his lips sealed in protest. His arms clamped tighter around his chest, then Elena realized he had his notebook tucked there against his heart.

"What is it?" Elena was losing her patience again, but she was also curious. What could he possibly have in there? And how could it have anything to do with what had happened on the front lawn that afternoon?

"We have to show her," Grace murmured, having her own private argument with Calvin. They battled quietly for a few more seconds before Grace's unblinking stubbornness won out and Calvin relented, loosening his arms. The notebook dropped and he caught it, thumbing through the pages and handing it off to Grace.

"We're here because of this," Grace said. And she came forward carefully, the notebook falling open to an ink drawing that spread out over the two pages.

Elena leaned forward to study it, taking in the sharp black lines that crisscrossed the paper forming shapes that her brain couldn't comprehend. Then the figures slowly began to swim into recognition, and Elena had to blink to make sure she wasn't seeing things.

"Is that Henry?" Her finger quivered as she reached out and tapped the page. "That's totally sadistic. Why would you draw that? Are you trying to be funny?"

Elena leapt to her feet, her anger pushing her out of her catatonic state. She rushed across the room and lifted Calvin's notebook high in one hand, ready to smack him with it. But then Grace jumped in the way, her hands held up to block the blow.

"He drew that *before* it happened."

Her words froze the blood in Elena's veins. She lowered the notebook slowly and took another look at the picture.

"W-what?" she stammered. "How?"

Everyone's eyes darted to Calvin, but his chin was buried in his chest, his glasses catching the light and reflecting it back in two impenetrable white discs.

"I don't know," Calvin finally muttered. "It's these visions— they pop into my head and take over. I have no idea where they come from. I just know that I have to draw them."

A minute stretched out and no one spoke.

"How long have you been able to do this?" Steph finally asked.

Calvin's eyes swiveled around the room, looking everywhere except at the three girls standing over him.

"This is useless," Elena sighed, rolling her eyes.

"I guess," Calvin squeaked, finally finding his voice. "I guess it all started about five years ago."

"And did you fall in a toxic vat of paint to get these pow- ers?" Elena scoffed. "Or I bet a group of monks injected you with a mystical vial of ink."

"It's not a joke," Grace said, coming to Calvin's defense. "I saw him drawing it. And I saw him try to warn you."

Elena pursed her lips, ready to tear this story apart.

"And this isn't the first time this has happened, is it?" Grace asked, turning to Calvin. "That day in the bleachers. You saw the volleyball hitting me in the face. You drew it and were able to push me out of the way in time. You were able to stop it."

Elena vaguely remembered that day, but she didn't share Grace's awe as Calvin nodded.

"The visions have always been terrible," Calvin croaked. "But that was the first time they'd ever come true."

"But why now?" Elena asked, not believing him for one second. She needed answers. Real ones. Not some made-up story about premonitions and magical mumbo-jumbo. "And how?"

This seemed to be the question on everyone's mind as they all turned apprehensively to Calvin.

"I—" Calvin paused and licked his lips. A bead of sweat slipped down his forehead before he could wipe it away. "I don't know. But the visions started after we played that game at your house, Elena."

Again, Elena had no clue what he was talking about.

"Bloody Mary," he replied in a reverent tone, his voice low as if he were afraid of invoking the name even now.

"You thought that was real?" Elena laughed. "We were nine. I was bored and trying to scare you. I made that whole thing up."

A tension fell over the room, uncomfortable and prickly as Calvin shook his head, unwilling to hear what Elena was saying, unwilling to accept it.

"What if you didn't?" Calvin frantically flipped through his notebook and held out another drawing, this one of a dreadfully beautiful woman. "Have you seen it?"

"No," Elena replied coolly.

But as she stared harder at the drawing, she couldn't help but feel something tapping at the back of her mind, lurking in her memory, at the edges of her dreams. A familiar voice, low and insistent, pulling her under. The ghastly face that she saw in her locker mirror.

The door swung open then and they all jumped. Calvin quickly slammed his notebook shut as they all turned to look up at their vice principal.

"Elena, we're ready for you."

Vice Principal Matthis's voice was stern and serious and didn't quite match his rumpled exterior. But she knew he meant business. One of his students was in the hospital.

"Whenever you're ready." And he turned and moved back into his office.

As Elena went to follow him, she cut a look at the other three.

"Fine," she murmured. "Meet me at my house after school and we can figure this out."

CHAPTER 16
STEPH

The kitchen was silent. No one knew what to say. They could only stare at one another from across the table, their notebooks and textbooks piled in front of them as if they were actually there for a study session.

In a way, though, it was a group project. They had research to do. Theories to postulate. A hypothesis to test. But how did they even start? How did they go about proving the existence of something impossible? Something supernatural? Something that frightened them all?

"What do you guys want on your pizza?" Elena's mom asked as she bustled into the room, her cell phone already out to make the call. "Pepperoni? Sausage? Vegetarian?"

"Whatever," Elena snapped.

"It's so good to see you four hanging out again," Elena's mom replied, ignoring her daughter.

"Mom," Elena said, bristling. "Just order the pizza and get out of here."

"All right. Well, I'll just get a margherita and a pepperoni. You all can fight over who gets what."

"Thanks," Steph said, feeling her stomach grumble even though Coach Lee had canceled practice that afternoon.

"It's not a problem." Elena's mom waved them off with a smile. "It should be here in thirty. I'll leave you all to it until then."

And Elena's mom made her way out of the kitchen, her phone dialing as she went.

"It was nice of your mom to drive us," Grace said, breaking her silence.

Elena's mom had picked them up after school. It had felt like they were nine years old all over again, getting shuttled around in their carpool. Steph's mom had been delighted to hear that she was going to a friend's house. And hearing her mom light up like that, Steph hadn't had the heart to correct her.

Elena was her teammate. Her co-captain. But definitely not her friend. And Steph was only here out of curiosity. She needed to get to the bottom of the vision that had clung to her for so many years. To understand why, now, this mirror girl had finally appeared in the flesh. As much as she wanted to deny it, there was a kind of magic there. Or maybe a curse.

"Let's see the drawing," Elena ordered, taking the lead as usual. Calvin's hands shook as he thumbed through his notebook and left the spread out in the middle of the table for all of them to see.

It was amazing how unfazed Elena seemed now as she scanned Calvin's picture. But then, the news had come back from the hospital during sixth period, phones vibrating in purses and pockets, students pulling them out without a care in the world. And for once, the teachers had looked the other way. Even they understood that this kind of news needed to be shared.

Henry was okay. He'd broken his arm and gotten ten stitches in his forehead, but he'd live. The doctors were holding him overnight, and he'd most likely be released in the morning. He was lucky.

"But what's this all supposed to mean?"

Elena already sounded frustrated and ready to give up. The drawing didn't shed any new light on what had happened that afternoon. It only showed an illustrated Elena yelling at Henry, her arms thrown up, his body tilting backward ever so slightly as a car came roaring into view at the edge of the paper.

"I don't know," Calvin replied weakly. "I draw what I see. What it shows me."

"It?"

Calvin flipped in his notebook to reveal a picture of a frightening thing with long, tangled hair. A demon.

"You've got to be kidding me," Elena scoffed. "You think

this—this *thing* pushed Henry into the street? Or was it driving the car?"

No one spoke. Not at first. But then—

"I believe him."

Steph grew suddenly shy, her voice shaky as everyone turned to look at her. She had even surprised herself when the words had come out of her mouth. But it was the truth, she realized. She had seen that awful face before, if even for just a split second. And now she knew she hadn't imagined it.

"I've seen it, too."

And as she admitted it, Steph felt a presence sweep into the room. Something dark and heavy, creeping along the walls. Something evil. A shiver ran up her spine, and she thought she smelled something like flowers. Only they were too sweet. Sickly, like they'd been left out a day or two past their prime.

"You all are crazy."

Elena's snarky retort snapped Steph out of her thoughts.

"You think that some invisible *thing* is haunting us?"

"It's a demon," Grace muttered. And even though it sounded crazy, the words hit home. Steph knew them to be true. Nothing about this really made sense.

"Well, this demon—or whatever you want to call it—it isn't in Calvin's drawing." Elena smirked, satisfied with her defense. "Unless I missed something."

At this, Calvin reached across the table and flipped back in his notebook. Steph pulled it close and studied it again.

Elena was right. It wasn't there. But something looked off. Steph squinted and brought the notebook within an inch of her nose.

"Calvin, did you finish this drawing?" Steph asked, hoping it didn't sound like a dumb question.

"I—" And Calvin froze as he thought. "I'm not sure."

"It's just—there are some faint lines here." Steph stretched across the table and pointed it out to Calvin. "Do you think you could complete it?"

Calvin stared at the page, his eyes wide.

"I don't know."

"Can you try?"

Steph held her breath, noticing the way Calvin's fingers trembled. She hoped she hadn't asked too much.

"I guess."

And he took the notebook from her. He studied the page, tapping it with the cap of the pen he'd pulled out of his pocket. He sucked in a deep breath, closed his eyes, and went still. His hand hovered in the air for a moment, and then, like the planchette on a Ouija board, it darted across the notebook, scratching new lines and details into the drawing. Elena's shirt gained its striped pattern. The expression of fear sharpened on Henry's face. The car's windshield blinked into focus, revealing the shadow of a driver. And then, right before their eyes, a figure emerged.

Its torn dress was unmistakable, its hair frightening in its

Medusa-like coils. Blood dripped from its lips as if it were preparing for a feast. It floated at Elena's back, a satisfied gleam in its eyes, a wicked smile contorting its mouth, its arms lifted high to mimic Elena's—or maybe to control them.

The room went quiet as Calvin's hand stilled. The sound of the pen scratching against the paper echoed in Steph's ears, the demon more terrifying than it'd looked in Calvin's other drawing. An uneasiness bubbled in her stomach and she felt that evil presence filling the room.

"Looks like you guys are working hard in here."

They all jumped as Elena's mom walked back into the kitchen, her eyes finding Calvin's notebook.

"Mom," Elena complained, her cheeks turning red.

"I was thirsty. Is it all right if I get something to drink?" She didn't wait for permission as she walked over to a cabinet and pulled out a cup. "Anyone else want something?"

They all shook their heads, watching as Elena's mom opened the fridge and poured herself a glass of iced tea.

"So what are you all working on?" she asked as she took a swig. "Got a big project on fairy tales or something?"

"Fairy tales?" Elena huffed, crossing her arms over her chest. "We're in high school, Mom."

"There's nothing wrong with fairy tales." Elena's mom clearly knew how to roll with the punches. She probably had lots of practice with Elena as her daughter. "That looks just like the ghost from one of your grandmother's old stories."

Elena's mom had come over to the table and was motioning down at Calvin's notebook.

"Don't you remember? It was your favorite one when you were little."

Steph's heart jumped as Elena's mom pointed right at the demon on the page.

"She was a fairy godmother." Then the woman's lips puckered and she put her finger to them. "Or maybe she was a witch? I can't remember the exact details. But it had something to do with finding your soulmate and being careful what you wished for. The price of true love and all that. You know, your typical cautionary tale."

Elena slow-blinked as Steph's heart skipped a beat.

"I'm surprised you don't remember. You made your grandma read it to you every time she visited."

"Mom," Elena seethed.

"I'm going, I'm going," Elena's mom promised as she choked on her tea and made her way out of the kitchen.

Then she was gone, which left the four of them exchanging inquisitive glances. First at the notebook, then at one another.

"We need to find that storybook," Steph said, looking directly at Elena.

CHAPTER 17
GRACE

They stood in a cluster outside the bedroom door, Grace tucked in tight next to Calvin, their arms brushing. She'd chosen the right day for her Velma getup. The four of them were in the middle of a real mystery. Only, Grace didn't think they'd find a man in a mask when they got to the bottom of it.

"What are we waiting for?" Elena huffed.

"I thought you were leading the way," Steph shot back.

A silent battle brewed between the two girls, their eyebrows furrowed in stubbornness.

"I'll do it."

And Grace surprised even herself as she pushed ahead of them all and grabbed the knob, the door hinges groaning in an eerie, cartoonish way. As a self-proclaimed queen of the night, this was kind of her element. She knew all the horror references, from camp to creature. She'd studied the classics like

Frankenstein, Dracula, and the Mummy, but had also binged all of *Buffy* and the Winchester brothers. If there were a demon or monster out there, she knew about it. She was prepared.

However, when the door swung open, Grace wasn't met by cobwebs in the corners or fog creeping along the floor hiding rats and snakes. There weren't any ghosts or bats or skeletons waiting for a jump scare. It was actually quite lovely. Cozy, even. The sun streamed in through the window and bathed the room in a warm, golden glow. And with the quilted blanket spread over the foot of the bed and a decorative arrangement of dried corn husks sitting in one corner, they could have walked into a bed-and-breakfast for how put together it all looked.

"My mom goes a little overboard," Elena said, wrinkling her nose as she picked a stuffed scarecrow doll off the bed and dropped it on the floor, flopping down to take its place on the mattress. "You should see it at Christmas—Santas and snow-men everywhere."

"Where's the storybook?" Grace got right to business. She glanced around the room but didn't see a bookcase. "Come on, I thought you wanted to figure this out."

Grace broke from her searching to shoot Elena a look, to which the girl harrumphed and then finally rolled off the bed. She got down on her knees and rummaged under the mattress for a few seconds before popping back up with a small wooden chest.

"My mom's been rearranging all week, getting her fall

decorations out," Elena said, opening the lid and pulling out a thick old tome. She handed it to Grace like it was no big deal and sat back down.

But to Grace, this book was everything. It was like discovering that million-dollar treasure at the flea market. The book was that good kind of heavy. With a leather-bound cover that looked expensive. When Grace opened it, the stiff pages crackled. But there wasn't a title or even a table of contents. As Grace flipped through it, though, she realized exactly what it was.

A story collection. A treasury of fairy tales, to be more specific, all of them accompanied by hand-painted illustrations. The pages were filled with princesses and witches and dragons and wolves. Bakers and spinning wheels and children who had lost their way.

"There," Steph spoke, her finger darting forward to pin the page. She and Calvin had come in close to peek over Grace's shoulder.

"That's her," Grace murmured, mesmerized by the picture, by the uncanny similarities it had to Calvin's. But it must have been a hundred years old. It didn't make sense.

"What story is this?" Grace wondered aloud as she flipped back in the book. "'Die Verflucht Frau'?"

She knew she'd butchered the pronunciation, and she suddenly realized that none of the stories were in English. The words had all the familiar letters, but they were arranged in new orders, with dots and dashes thrown in over some of them.

She tried sounding out the title again and failed just as miserably as the first time.

"It's German," Elena explained like it should have been obvious. And Grace could have kicked herself. Of course. The Germans basically invented the fairy tale. They knew how to do dark and creepy.

"Can you read it for us?" Steph asked.

"Does it look like I speak German?" Elena rolled to a sitting position but didn't get up.

"Do you at least remember what this story was about?"

Grace turned the book around to show her, but Elena didn't seem very interested. So she pulled it back and started flipping through the pages, searching the illustrations for some context.

In the first, a maiden stood in front of a mirror, her reflection glowing with youth and beauty. Her long hair cascaded over her back in golden waves and her skin gave off a pearly aura. She could have been a princess or an evil stepsister—anything, really.

In the next, a serving girl was bent at the woman's feet. The woman looked just as radiant, but this time there was something else lurking in the mirror, a shadow that the woman didn't seem to be aware of as she gazed at her own reflection. But the maid had noticed, her eyes fixed on the mirror even as she straightened the maiden's dress.

And then in the third picture, the shadow in the mirror came into focus. The demon from Calvin's drawing filled the whole page, every gruesome detail rendered in startling clarity. Grace could see the desire in its eyes, the blood staining its canine teeth. It was ghastly and hungry and evil.

Grace quickly turned the page, and there was one last illustration. But this one puzzled her the most.

The maiden had disappeared completely from the scene, and now the serving girl stood with her back to the mirror, her clothes changed from rough burlap to colorful silk. Her hair done up beautifully. Her face glowing.

But there was something off about the drawing. Grace couldn't put her finger on it until . . . there, on the ground behind the serving girl. A trail of blood led right to the mirror. Were they footprints? Or droplets? And were they going to the mirror? Or coming out of it?

Grace squinted and saw the flicker of something in the mirror's reflection. It could have been the serving girl's shadow. Or it could just as easily have been the demon waiting to claim her next prize.

"Well?" Steph asked, jarring Grace out of her thoughts.

"I—" Grace tried to think it out. "I think it's something to do with vanity. Mirrors and being drawn in by your own reflection. But without the translation, I can't know for sure. It's definitely dark. But it wouldn't be a German fairy tale without a little bloodshed."

"We can at least look up the title," Steph suggested.

Of course. That would help. Grace fumbled to get her

phone out while also holding on to the book, then quickly typed in the German words. "Die Verflucht Frau."

"'The Cursed Woman,'" she read aloud, her voice trembling slightly, the words knocking the room into an eerie silence.

"So what now?" Calvin asked after a few moments, and Grace was surprised to see that he and Steph were looking to her.

"Well . . ." Grace cast around for an idea. And her eyes fell on the shrouded piece of furniture across the room. "I guess we should start with the mirror. Did everyone see something that day? When we played Elena's game? It was supposed to reveal our soulmates, right?"

"I saw Henry," Elena announced, perking up at the change in conversation. "Which makes total sense because we've been together for three years."

"You *were* together," Steph corrected her.

"Do you think that's why he got hurt?" Grace gasped. "Because you broke up?"

Elena's expression soured, but before she could snap a retort, Grace had gone on.

"No, that wouldn't make sense because I'm not with—" And then she froze, realizing that she was thinking out loud.

"You're not with who?" Elena pressed, a gleeful smirk raising the corners of her mouth. "Who'd *you* see in the mirror that day?"

"I saw—" Grace's face flushed at the thought of confessing. But she couldn't hide it. Not if they wanted to get to the bottom of this. "I saw Calvin."

Her ears burned. She couldn't look at him. Couldn't bear to see if he was surprised or—

"And who did you see, Calvin?" Elena took the reins, enjoying herself now.

"I—" Calvin struggled to get the words out, which only made Grace feel worse. He hadn't seen her. They weren't meant to be. She wasn't his soulmate.

"I didn't see a person," Calvin finally managed to get out. "I saw *her.*"

It was like a lightning bolt had struck the center of the room, stunning them all with the revelation.

He'd seen it. The demon. He'd seen death. Which meant . . .

A lump formed in Grace's throat.

Was that why he had the visions? Why he saw danger everywhere he looked? He was seeing and drawing all these disasters, these accidents hurting the people around him. And eventually, he'd draw his own.

She wanted to reach out and give him a hug. She wanted to assure him that they'd figure a way out of this. They'd stop this curse. They'd save him.

But how could she guarantee that? Would her empty promises mean anything? Especially now that he knew she'd seen his face in the mirror. That she liked him. That she'd had a crush on him for the past five years.

The lump in Grace's throat swelled, and this time she couldn't swallow it down. She could only stand in silence and worry.

"Last but not least," Elena chirped in a singsong voice. "Who did you see, Steph?"

"I—" Steph faltered, and Grace worried she might have seen the demon, too. "I saw Cody Crosby."

"Didn't his family move away last year?" Elena asked, clearly disappointed in Steph's answer, though Grace didn't know what else she would have expected.

Steph nodded, her eyes downcast as she worried at her bottom lip.

"I barely knew him," she eventually said, shrugging. "So I never put much thought into it."

That left them at another dead end.

"So if it wasn't actually showing us our soulmates . . ." Grace wouldn't let the mystery stump her yet. "What *did* it do?"

She turned her attention to the mirror, still covered by its sheet, standing by itself in the corner of the room. She took a few steps toward it, feeling the air chill around her, an uncomfortable prickle crawling like a spider up her neck.

But she also felt its pull—a pulse beckoning her to come closer.

"What are you doing?" Elena sounded panicked all of a sudden.

"Isn't this what we're here to see?" Grace asked. And before Elena could get out another word of protest, she'd grabbed the sheet and tugged.

They all watched as the shroud unfurled in a rush of sliding linen. But when the mirror came into full view, a collective gasp ran through the room.

"It's cracked," Grace murmured, turning to Elena. And for once, Elena didn't have a snappy reply at the ready.

"It wasn't my fault—"

Grace wasn't listening, though. She'd turned back to inspect the mirror. But she could only see the gaping hole, the void right where her heart would be reflected.

"It was an accident. I didn't mean to—" Elena sputtered, losing steam.

"When?" Grace asked, her voice surprisingly calm.

"I don't know. Maybe a week ago?"

Grace nodded, absorbing the new detail, adding it to the mystery.

Other than the crack, the mirror looked exactly as she remembered it. Ornate and old. Sturdy. A silver filigree swooped around the mirror's face with pearls inset into the pattern. But as Grace got closer to the frame to really examine it, she saw that the silver wasn't a decorative border at all.

It was a script. Actual words, though not in any language or alphabet she recognized.

She ran her fingers along the lines, feeling the bumps of the looping letters, how they curved and coiled around the mirror's face like a snake. There was something familiar about them, but she couldn't figure out what.

"Let me take a picture of these," Grace said as she stood up.

She pulled out her phone and centered the camera on the mirror. Then she came in close, getting shots of the script, making sure she got all of it.

When she stepped back, though, something wasn't right. A strange aura had invaded every picture, wrapping the mirror and the words in dark shadows, an impenetrable fog.

Grace scrolled back and forth through her photo gallery, sure that there was something wrong with her eyes or with the camera lens. She even took a test shot of her feet and then pointed the phone back up at the mirror. The white laces of her shoes came back crystal clear, but again, the picture of the mirror was completely blurred out.

"Can I borrow some paper?" Grace asked. Calvin didn't waste any time as he tore a page from the back of his notebook and handed it to her along with his pen.

Grace startled at how heavy the writing utensil felt in her hand. Heavy and cold. A weapon. A knife with its pointed tip. And wasn't it just as dangerous? At least in Calvin's fingers?

She shook the thought from her head and focused back on the mirror, plopping onto the floor and getting to work. She copied the symbols down as quickly as she could. Elena's mom would call for them soon, and she wanted to make sure she got this right. She just knew that the words held the key to figuring this whole thing out.

And if she could decode them, then maybe—just maybe—she could save Calvin.

CHAPTER 18
CALVIN

A pile of papers lay scattered on the floor of Grace's bedroom, like autumn leaves just dropped from their branches. They crackled as she picked through them, her tongue stuck out in concentration.

"I've been doing a ton of research," Grace explained as she shuffled through more of her notes. She looked so in her element, and it impressed Calvin that she'd pulled together so much in only a couple of days.

"There are a ton of superstitions around mirrors," Grace went on. "They can be used to summon spirits and to see the future. They're doorways between our world and the next. They can steal souls. Suck them right out of our bodies. And they can even be used to foreshadow someone's death."

She paused then, her face paling as her eyes darted up to meet Calvin's.

"It's okay," Calvin assured her.

And it really was. He'd had this fate looming over his head for almost five years now. The visions and the drawings. He'd gotten used to it all. Grown tired of it. And had even, in a way, come to accept it.

"I've also been looking into Elena's grandmother's story," Grace picked back up, choosing her words more carefully now. "Trying to find its origin and a translation. Obviously, Germany was my first thought, but I couldn't find anything. Not when I searched for 'Die Verflucht Frau.' And not with anything else I tried."

"Maybe it's original," Calvin suggested. He'd thought a lot about that book, the hand-painted illustrations and the fact that it didn't have a title. About how old it looked. "It could be part of a family collection. Something passed down from generation to generation."

"I was thinking that, too," Grace agreed. "I just need to see it again so I can translate it. But who knows if Elena will even hand it over. You heard her. She thinks this is all a joke."

Elena had seemed pretty dismissive when they'd left her house the other night. She thought Calvin had made it all up. Or that he had something wrong with his brain. But he knew he wasn't crazy. Finding this connection had proven that. It had given him hope. If they could only piece it all together.

"Have you made any progress on that mirror language?" Calvin asked as he picked up the page that had come out of his own notebook. He studied the script that Grace had copied down. She had a steady hand. She could probably make a good artist on her own. He traced his finger along the smooth loops as if that could somehow let him understand it.

"Another dead end," Grace sighed. "But I got some solid leads. It looks kind of like something I found in this old grimoire online."

Calvin cocked an eyebrow.

"It's like a textbook," Grace explained. "But for magic. It has incantations and summonings and spells and rituals. I ordered one online that seemed promising, but I won't know until it gets here."

Grace fell silent then, her shoulders sagging as she exhausted her research. Calvin didn't like how defeated she looked. She'd already done so much. None of them could have gotten half as far.

"Maybe Elena will come around." Calvin tried to sound optimistic. "Or she'll remember something her grandmother said."

Grace huffed out a stream of air. "I doubt it."

"Didn't you used to be friends?" Calvin asked, curiosity getting the better of him. "I just—I remember you two were always whispering when we used to carpool together."

"We were close," Grace replied, her hand sneaking up to her chest, pulling at the locket around her neck, which Calvin had come to recognize as a nervous tic.

"What happened?"

"I'm not really sure." Grace's eyes lost their focus suddenly, turned distant.

"You don't have to—"

"It's fine," she went on, even though she looked anything but fine. "Elena and I *were* friends. Best friends. But then after my mom—after she was gone—Elena just disappeared. She abandoned me, too, right when I needed her the most."

Calvin felt the wind knocked out of him. He hadn't realized that the two losses were connected. He hadn't even known for certain that Grace's mom had died in that car accident until Grace had mentioned it a couple of weeks ago. But to lose her best friend right after going through that—it was criminal.

"I don't know if I wasn't cool enough," Grace continued, "or if my sadness was too much for her to handle. It doesn't really matter. I stopped hearing from her and that was that."

"I wish I had known," Calvin replied.

But Grace only shrugged. "You probably wouldn't have liked me back then. I was sad all the time."

Grace sighed, her shoulders dipping again. She still didn't look happy, but at least the tears had cleared from her eyes.

"But now I know not to put too much faith in anyone. Because you never know when they'll decide to leave you."

It sounded bleak, but Calvin couldn't blame her.

"You can count on me," he assured her. "I'm not going anywhere."

But even this, Calvin realized too late, was a lie. He had no idea how much longer he had left. Each day could be his last. And it looked like Grace knew that, too.

"Here, I want to show you something." Calvin held out his hands for Grace to stay put while he got to his feet and grabbed his bag. He quickly fished out his notebook and flipped to the back of it.

"Trying to cheer me up with your death drawings?"

"No. These aren't those drawings. They're mine."

And Calvin opened the notebook to show her, turning the pages slowly so she could see.

"These," Grace stammered as she fingered the corners of the pages. "These are amazing."

Calvin had to hide his own smile at her glee. "It's your Wolf Man."

Grace tapped the picture excitedly. He'd known she'd like that one.

"And that's not all."

Calvin held his breath as he flipped the page. He'd finished it late the night before.

"You—" Grace gasped, her eyes darting from the page to Calvin. "You drew this for me?"

"Unless you know of another Elvira fan."

Calvin couldn't contain his grin this time. He'd had to look up the horror hostess because he had no idea who she was. But he'd seen her on enough of Grace's T-shirts to know she was one of her idols. Once he had a few references, it'd been pretty easy to draw Grace in the woman's likeness.

"So I take it you're a fan?"

"I love it!" Grace screeched. She flung her arms around Calvin's neck. "Can I have it?"

And Calvin nodded, carefully tearing the picture out of his notebook.

"You have to sign it first," Grace insisted, which threw Calvin off.

He'd never had to do that before. Did he sign his whole name or just his initials? He'd seen artists do it both ways. Unsure, he quickly decided on a combination and squiggled a *C* and then his last name in the bottom corner. He handed it off to Grace and she leapt to her feet, padding across the room to her desk where she pinned it proudly on her bulletin board.

"My very own Calvin Lee original." She beamed back at him. "Hopefully the first of many."

And then, before either of them could get caught up in what she'd just said, Grace bounded back and sat down next to him.

"You know, you should do this at the carnival. Set up an easel and everything. I bet a lot of people would pay to have their own monster caricature."

"But we're going to the carnival together," Calvin replied. He didn't want to abandon her on opening night. And he wasn't sure that he was ready for so many people to see his work. He couldn't control his visions. He never had any idea when they'd hit. The last thing he wanted was to hand someone a picture of a roller coaster crash or a finger lost on the Tilt-A-Whirl or a corn dog stick to the eye or a fun-house fire.

"Promise you'll think about it," Grace insisted. "I know it's scary. Maybe you can do a bunch of random monsters before and sell them during the carnival. That way you won't have to draw on the spot."

"I'll think about it," Calvin replied.

"People need to see what you can do. You're so talented."

And Calvin had to take a moment to collect himself. To breathe. No one had ever believed in him like this. No one had ever cared so much about him. He'd shared the scariest parts of himself and Grace hadn't run away. She'd embraced him. She was doing everything she could to save him.

"There's something else you should see," Calvin said slowly, deciding that he could trust her. He flipped back in his note-book, fingering the pages, thinking carefully before he pulled out three sheets of paper and laid them out in front of Grace.

"What are these?" Grace asked as she bent close. And then she gasped.

"It's us," Calvin said, pointing to each picture in succession. "Elena, Steph, and you."

"But when did you draw these?" Grace hadn't looked up from the pages.

"At the beginning of the month," Calvin replied. "But I didn't want to show anyone. I wasn't sure what they meant."

"Is this Henry's accident?"

Grace pointed to the picture of Elena, a close-up of her face, her eyes wide with horror, her mouth open in a scream that Calvin could hear ripping off the page. Flecks of blood dotted her cheeks, and Calvin suddenly realized that Grace was right. It was from the accident, Henry's blood speckled across Elena's face. A premonition drawn weeks before it had happened.

"Have the others come true yet?"

Grace's question brought Calvin out of his thoughts. His eyes darted to the other drawings—Steph with what looked like fireworks shooting off around her head, her eyes clenched shut in terror, and Grace surrounded by hundreds of shards of broken glass, blood dripping from her palm down to her elbow.

"I don't think so." Calvin's voice wobbled. Why did he have to be the bearer of bad news? This demon's harbinger of doom?

"Don't worry," Grace said, reaching out, stilling his trembling hands with her own. "We'll figure this out before anything else happens. Before anyone else gets hurt."

Calvin nodded and tried to take heart in Grace's certainty. But he couldn't help thinking about the fourth picture from that series—the one he'd kept tucked away inside his notebook. It would have frightened Grace more. And she didn't need to see that. No one did.

CHAPTER 19
ELENA

The sliding glass door whooshed open in front of Elena, startling her out of her stupor. She took a few steps back and swore under her breath. She hadn't pressed the call button. But was someone watching? Was there a time limit? She'd only been standing there for five minutes. It wasn't loitering—

Then a nurse in blue scrubs appeared, friendly as could be, nothing at all like the hospital bouncer Elena had feared. She relaxed, watching him disappear down the hallway, and when she turned back to the ward, the door had whooshed shut again, leaving her alone with her reflection, unsure of what to do.

Did she really want to see him? Did she even know what she was going to say? Would he be angry? Would he blame her for what had happened?

In the glass door, Elena watched the get-well balloon bob

lazily over her head, its toothy, bright-yellow smiley face the stuff of nightmares. Her gaze slipped to her face. She felt a tug in her gut, like she might tip forward and fall headfirst into herself, get sucked into her own eyes and lost forever.

You don't owe him anything.

She blinked and came out of her daze, noticing how she teetered on her tiptoes. She shook her head and tried to clear her thoughts.

She did owe Henry.

Her phone chirped, and Elena fought the urge to pull it out. It'd only be from her anonymous admirer, checking in like he did every few hours, asking if she was okay, telling her that the accident wasn't her fault, that she shouldn't beat herself up about it or listen to the rumors swirling around at school.

She didn't need his assurances, though. They didn't really do her any good. She needed to see Henry. To check on him. To make sure he really was okay. She needed to clear her conscience. So, steeling herself, Elena reached forward and pressed the call button, the door sliding open again to let her into the hospital ward.

Elena approached the front desk and smiled a thanks as a nurse pointed her in the right direction. She took her time getting to Henry's room, pausing outside the door. Nerves fluttered in her stomach—like this was a first date or something—and she didn't know why. This was Henry. She didn't need to impress him.

But still, she hoped she looked all right. She hadn't known what to wear to an ex-boyfriend's hospital bed. She hadn't wanted to look like she was trying, but then she hadn't wanted to look casual either.

So she'd gone with a post-practice ensemble. Matching sweatpants and jacket in their school colors. That way he'd know she was adding this to the end of her day instead of dropping everything to see him. She'd kept her hair in a ponytail, but she had thrown a dusting of makeup on her cheeks and applied a nude lip gloss. She smacked her lips, tightened her hair, and knocked.

"Oh, Elena."

Elena was thrown by the sight of Henry's mom at the door. Henry's mom, who'd always had fresh cookies waiting when they had hung out at his house. Who'd always made a point of including Elena when Henry and his younger brother got caught up in video game and baseball talk. Who'd actually taken her side in a couple of the fights she and Henry had had over the years, winking slyly and saying that girls had to stick together when boys were being dumb. What must she think of Elena now?

"Did you want to come in?"

Elena remembered herself then and pasted on a smile. "I just wanted to see how he was doing. Is that okay?"

She hated that her voice quivered. That she felt the need to ask permission.

"Of course," Henry's mom said as she moved aside and let Elena slip in. "I was actually just running to get some tea, so you two can talk while I'm gone."

And with that, Henry's mom grabbed her purse and stole out of the room, leaving Elena and Henry all by themselves.

The hospital room had an unsettling quiet to it, the silence punctuated by the intermittent beeps of what Elena assumed was Henry's heart monitor. She watched the graph peak and die down, its steady rhythm comforting, allowing her to relax and focus on the body lying in the bed.

Except for the stitches and cast, Henry could have been Sleeping Beauty. The way his dark hair fell over his forehead, Elena wanted to reach out and push it back, feel its soft brush again. It was something she hadn't realized she'd missed in the week since their breakup.

"What are you looking at?" Henry croaked, startling Elena as his eyes fluttered open. "I'm kind of surprised you came."

"Henry," Elena sputtered. "How are you feeling?"

"Don't worry. It looks worse than it is."

And now, with him awake, Elena realized how bad it actually did look. His arm was bound in a cast that went all the way to his shoulder. And she noticed the row of stitches on his forehead now that he'd pushed his hair back, his pale complexion and the purple rings around both his eyes.

"Four hours of surgery," Henry explained, and Elena quickly blinked away from his cast. "A shattered humerus, the funniest bone in the body. They said it was like a jigsaw puzzle putting it back together."

He forced a laugh then, but Elena couldn't find the humor to match it.

"I know, it's cheesy. But for some reason I thought it was hilarious when the doctor said it. Probably the painkillers."

An awkward silence fell over the room, something that never would have happened a week ago.

"Henry . . ." Elena started and then stopped, still unsure of what to say. "Are you really going to be okay?"

"I'm going to need a lot of rehab and I'll probably have to start wearing my hair down." Henry paused, and this time Elena was able to muster a smile. "But I'm all right. I promise. Still in one piece and expected to make a full recovery."

At that, Elena's shoulders unclenched and her whole body relaxed. She hadn't realized she'd been carrying around so much anxiety.

"Are you still mad at me?" she asked, relieved as she slipped back into that comfortable pattern that she and Henry had always had.

"Funny enough, I think I'm actually over it." Henry seemed to surprise even himself. "You know, getting hit by a car kind of puts things in perspective. And I think I've learned that it's dangerous to get on your bad side."

"I hope you know that it wasn't me," Elena rushed to say, her face suddenly hot with guilt. "I didn't—"

"Elena." Henry stopped her, his hand finding hers on the bed and squeezing it gently. "I was joking. We were together for three years. I know what you are and aren't capable of."

She breathed easier. At least Henry knew that she wasn't a monster. Unlike those nasty rumors at school trying to convince everyone that she'd seen the car coming. That she'd purposely pushed Henry out into traffic. Elena hadn't realized she had so many enemies. So many people ready to tear her down. But as long as Henry knew the truth, she could deal with the rest.

"I must have slipped off the curb or something," Henry assured her. "I know you would never hurt me like that."

"I'm still sorry," Elena said. "About everything."

And in that *everything*, she hoped Henry understood.

"It's been weird not having you around," Henry said. "My whole family misses you."

"They do?"

"Well, mostly my little brother," Henry clarified.

"Martin?"

He nodded. "I think he has a crush on you. Couldn't you tell?"

Elena shrugged and then laughed, Henry joining in with her. And it felt good. Normal. Like old times. Like they were always meant to be. Like it'd been fated.

"Have you ever wondered why we got together?"

The question had popped into Elena's head and she couldn't

help asking it. She didn't believe the ghost story Grace, Calvin, and Steph were trying to sell her, but a part of her did wonder. She'd been nine when she looked into that mirror, so she couldn't say for sure if she'd seen anything at all. She'd had a crush on Henry back then, and as the memory had faded, she'd started assuming that she had imagined him there. She'd seen who she wanted to see.

"You didn't really give me an option." Henry chuckled and then winced as he clutched at his injured arm.

"Should I call a nurse?" Elena leaned forward, worried.

"No. It's fine. Just a little tender when I move it."

His arm dropped and the grimace cleared from his face.

"Do you remember how you asked me out?" Henry eased right back into Elena's question.

"I wrote you that ridiculous note," she recalled after a moment, suddenly embarrassed by her younger self. "With the boxes for you to check. *Will you go out with me? Yes. No. Maybe.* It sounds so silly now."

"It was cute," Henry insisted, getting a kick out of the memory. "And you're forgetting that you only left one option for me to check. *Yes. Yes.* And *Yes.* I literally couldn't say no."

"I knew what I wanted. And you clearly were into it since you checked all three *Yes*es."

"I guess I really liked you."

And there it was. She knew it by the way his words echoed in her ears. The hollowness of his tone. The past tense of that sentence. She smiled to herself because it was the only way to keep from crying.

It was just, sometimes she wondered if soulmates were real. Like, what if they were meant to be and now they'd ruined their opportunity? What if he was her one and only, just like the mirror had foretold?

She wanted to ask him, but she knew she couldn't. She'd look so stupid. Especially after she'd been the one talking to someone else. After she'd been the one to break them up.

It's not your fault.

Don't let him make you feel less than.

You're better off on your own.

The whispers came from all over, glinting off stethoscopes and IV drips. The blackened TV screen. The sliver of mirror showing through the open bathroom door. The computer monitors and shiny linoleum floor and bottles of medicine.

A chill crept through her body, reaching into her chest and squeezing her heart in an icy vise as the whispers grew louder, as they poured into her ears and overwhelmed her. She wanted to scream. They were too much to listen to. Too strong to ignore.

He was never good enough for you.

He's not the one.

Don't waste your time on him.

She couldn't fight it. Couldn't quiet the voices. A shadow appeared at the edge of her vision, taking its time coming into focus, preparing to step into the light, to meet her head-on. But Elena wasn't ready. She didn't want to see. She couldn't—

"Look," Henry began, reading into Elena's sudden quiet. "We had a good run. Three years. It's more than anyone could have expected. Maybe even more than we deserved. It's probably better that we broke up instead of drawing it out."

Elena felt a strange lightness settle in her. He really was over her. He'd moved on, as simple as that.

"But I am worried about you."

She stiffened as Henry went on.

"You always go after what you want, and I really admire that about you. But this girl you've become—this girl who goes behind people's backs, who flirts with strange boys she's never even met, who starts fights in the hallways at school— that's not someone I recognize. It's not you. You're better than that."

There's nothing wrong with going after what you want.

That is who you are.

The voices flooded back in, filling her mind, stoking her anger, tempering her words.

It's like he doesn't know you at all.

"Maybe you're wrong," Elena snapped. "Maybe I *am* that girl. Maybe I need to be strong to get what I want. To get what I deserve. To make sure no one takes it from me."

Henry looked taken aback, but he quickly recovered, biting out his own reply.

"If you have to be mean and use tricks to get it, then did you really deserve it in the first place?"

Anger sparked in Elena's stomach and surged through her whole body, the creeping cold from before disappeared in a flash of flame. Her hands began shaking.

"Next time, try looking both ways before you cross the street. Or don't."

And with that, she turned and stormed out, all thoughts of soulmates burned to ash in her mind.

CHAPTER 20
STEPH

When the last-bus bell rang, echoing down the freshman hall, Steph was the only one there to hear it. But for once, she wasn't in a hurry. She took her time gathering the books she needed for homework, all the while trying not to think about the demon that may or may not be real. That may or may not have cursed her.

Instead, she tried to focus on that night's game. If one thing could help her forget, it was volleyball. And tonight they were playing their district rivals, which meant they had to win. She couldn't afford any distractions.

What about your soulmate?

The thought flitted to Steph's ear, like a butterfly alighting on a flower, its wings batting, tickling, flirtatious.

You can't forget about her.

And before Steph knew it, she found herself leaning up against her locker, sinking into a daydream.

Thoughts of the new girl filled her head. Steph still didn't know her name. She hadn't worked up the courage to approach her on her own. But she'd seen her in the halls, spied on her in the cafeteria. She'd talk to her eventually. She just had to find the right time. The perfect moment.

"Hey there."

Steph snapped upright, the voice surprising her, and she banged the back of her head against the locker.

"Oh my gosh, are you all right?"

Someone rushed forward and laid a hand on Steph's shoulder, which only made Steph swoon harder as she realized it was the new girl standing in front of her, as if Steph had somehow conjured her from her thoughts.

"Sorry. I didn't mean to scare you."

"I'm fine," Steph assured her, feeling guilty for making her worry.

"Good," the girl replied, leaving Steph speechless. She didn't want the girl to go, but she didn't know how to keep her there either.

"I'm Steph."

The introduction popped out of her mouth, and she hoped she didn't sound silly or too forward.

"It's nice to meet you," the girl said, reaching a hand out for a shake. "I'm Mary."

Mary.

It echoed in Steph's head. Just like the thing in the mirror.

Only this was a girl. Steph's dream girl. Maybe even her soulmate. There wasn't anything demonic about her. No devil horns. No blood dripping from the corner of her mouth. She didn't hiss when she spoke. There was no way this girl was evil. And now, finally, Steph had a name to put to that face. Those features she couldn't help but be drawn to.

Now that she had the girl up close, Steph could see the finer details. The light freckles dusting the bridge of her nose. The golden tones glittering in her short brown hair. The ink stains left on the tips of her index and middle fingers. The ease she seemed to have in her own skin. The confidence.

"I know who you are," Mary said.

And Steph jolted out of her daze, suddenly wondering if this girl might have had visions of her, too. Had she seen the demon?

"You're our star volleyball player." Mary said it like it was common knowledge. "Some girls in my bio class were talking about how good you are."

Steph blushed from her neck all the way up to her forehead. That people would talk about her. That a girl like Mary would take notice and remember.

"You all have a game tonight, right?"

"Yeah," Steph managed to jump back in. And then, in what might have been the bravest moment of her life, she asked the unthinkable. "Actually, you should come. See me in action. See if I live up to the hype."

Even as Steph held her breath, her heart pounding in her chest, wondering what spirit had taken over her body to make her say something so bold, she realized that it was the right move. Because if there was one place where she excelled, where she lost her awkward tallness and anxiety, it was on the volleyball court. If she wanted to impress this girl, the only place she'd be able to do it was there.

"Sure. I can check it out."

And Steph had to blink to make sure she'd heard right.

"It's at six?"

Mary stopped walking, bending over to fiddle with a bike lock. And Steph realized that they'd made it all the way out to the front of the school. How had she not noticed that?

"Yeah. The game starts at six." Steph's own words echoed in her ears.

"Great. I'll see you tonight." Mary mounted her bike and snapped a helmet over her head. "Good luck. I'll be cheering for you."

And with that farewell, Mary coasted away, disappearing without a backward glance. Which was okay with Steph, because that meant she could stare at her without being seen.

CHAPTER 21
GRACE

The stands were packed that night, even for the freshman game, which went on first. The crowd buzzed with a frantic kind of energy, pushing in, filling up the space, spilling over so that Grace could barely handle it. Her toes tapped uncontrollably beneath her, her locket out and squeezed between her lips as she watched the court.

Her eyes flicked to either side, to spectators chomping on nachos and popcorn and hot dogs, tossing chips and kernels into their mouths without a care in the world. But what if one of them were only a bite away from choking to death?

Grace blinked and her gaze slipped to the bleachers, the wood worn and creaking. Could this many jostling fans cause a support to collapse? To send them all tumbling down into a deadly pit of metal rods, splinters, and sawdust?

She closed her eyes, but it didn't stop the worry from

burning through her, the anxiety from driving her mad.

Was this how Calvin felt every single day?

After hanging out with him, his power had kind of rubbed off on her. She didn't see images or anything, but she understood the paranoia that riddled him. She couldn't stop imagining the worst everywhere she looked. She didn't know how he managed it all.

On the court, Steph suddenly leapt up to block a ball, and Grace couldn't help but wince, hiding behind her hands in case the net cord snapped and cut off one of the girl's fingers. Grace thought of Calvin's drawings—the three he'd done of them. Elena's had come true, which left Steph's and Grace's. Luckily there weren't any fireworks set to go off in the gym, but that didn't mean they shouldn't keep their eyes open. Disaster could be lurking around every corner. Calvin had taught her that.

"Did I miss something?"

Grace jumped. But then her shoulders relaxed as she recognized Calvin's voice there beside her.

"You're back," Grace said, surprised at how relieved she felt.

"And I got sodas."

Calvin held up the two drinks and handed one over as he settled onto the bleacher next to her. They were pretty close to the floor. Only a few rows up. Which made for a great view. But more importantly, a quick exit in case all hell broke loose.

Which it wouldn't.

But it could.

And Grace wanted to be prepared. Just in case.

"How are they doing?" Calvin asked, and Grace realized that she hadn't been paying attention. Her eyes darted over to the scoreboard hanging on the wall behind the court, and she quickly read off the numbers.

"Twenty to fifteen," she exclaimed, as if he couldn't have seen it himself. "Looks like we're going to win this set."

"That'll put my mom in a good mood." Calvin nodded as he took a sip of his soda and shuffled closer to her.

Grace couldn't help but notice the careful way he repositioned his notebook on his knee, his palm resting on the leather cover, almost caressing it. It was such a natural movement. He probably didn't even realize he did it. Like an addiction that caused him so much suffering but that he couldn't live without.

"Are you feeling okay?" Grace asked, seeing a slight quiver in Calvin's index finger. A tug at the corner of his brow.

"I'm fine," Calvin replied. But Grace could tell something was off.

"Here, let me hold on to that for you."

She reached out to take the notebook, but Calvin's fingers balled into a fist, pressing down on the sketch pad, trapping it against his thigh.

"You can't."

"I can help you," Grace insisted.

And she could, she suddenly realized. If he'd only let her.

Why hadn't she thought of it sooner? She could save him

right here and now. If he didn't have his notebook, then he couldn't draw the terrible visions that plagued him. And maybe that would be enough to prevent disaster from striking. To save them all.

"I'm saying it won't work," Calvin tried to explain.

"But—" Grace pressed, wanting to defend her idea, to make it true.

"The visions come out whether I have my notebook or not. I can keep them at bay for a little while, but if I'm not ready—"

Calvin shuddered, and Grace didn't want to hear the end of his story. But she had to know.

"If you're not ready . . . what happens?"

"They find other ways—" Calvin swallowed hard, fighting the memory. But then his chin dipped in surrender. "When I can't hold it back anymore, the visions take over. I black out and when I come to, it's there. It's there no matter what I do. Drawn in whatever ink and on whatever paper I can find."

And by the way Calvin stared at his palms, transfixed by the lines pumping blood in and out of his hand, Grace knew exactly what kind of ink the demon found to use.

"Calvin, I'm so sorry," she whispered, her hand finding his and then jerking back at the icy cold touch, as if a spirit had already come in to possess it.

Luckily, a roar burst from the crowd right then and Grace was able to turn her attention back to the game. Steph had just spiked the ball for a kill off a perfect set from Elena, and they had their first set point. Grace followed the rest of the crowd and rose to her feet, shouting and waving her hands out in front of her, doing everything in her power not to look over at Calvin. Not to think about all the grim things he'd seen.

Instead, Grace focused on Steph, the crowd going quiet when she served, holding a collective breath as the point played out.

The ball went back and forth, both teams getting digs and putting up partial blocks. Grace cheered "PI-O-NEERS!" with the rest of the fans each time their team touched the ball. It was the longest point of the match, and Grace couldn't help but get swept up in it, pulled along by the pulse-pounding moment. She peeked to the side, ready to celebrate this nail-biter with Calvin, but he wasn't there. He wasn't standing, at least. He was still hunched over on the bleachers, his pen scratching away in his lap, filling the notebook that he'd flipped open.

"Calvin?"

Panic sank its fangs into Grace and sucked all the blood right out of her. It left her cold and light-headed and completely out of sorts. The crowd swam around her, the game suddenly suspended in slow motion. She squinted and tried to see what Calvin was drawing, but his head blocked out the images. She had to see, though. She had to know what was going to happen. She had to stop it if she could. She had to save them.

"Calvin!" Grace screamed his name this time and grabbed his shoulder. She yanked him back, gritting her teeth, steeling herself for whatever disaster had visited him. She squinted, but couldn't make out the drawing. Couldn't make out the straight lines. The stars flying out in every direction. The fireworks shooting up from the ground.

"Steph!" Grace shrieked, her brain finally piecing it all together.

As she swung forward to scream again, she accidentally knocked the notebook out of Calvin's scribbling hands and onto the gym floor. But she didn't have time to worry about that, about who might see his deepest secrets. The dark thoughts that plagued him.

She had to get to Steph. She had to—

The crowd groaned as Steph dove for a ball, her whole body laid out on the floor at the back of the court. She wasn't able to handle it, though, and it ricocheted off her arms, flying like a bullet, slamming right into the scoreboard hanging on the wall above her.

An explosion like a cluster of cherry bomb firecrackers went off, and the scoreboard lights flickered. They dimmed and then blinked back too bright, throbbing like a pair of eyes about to pop out of their sockets.

And then they did.

The numbers exploded, sending a shower of sparks and pulverized glass down over Steph, who was still sprawled out on the floor.

People started screaming as Steph threw her arms over her

face. Then a metallic shriek ripped through the gym and the scoreboard lurched free of the wall. It caught for a second, hovering over Steph's head just before she was able to roll out of the way, and then it succumbed to gravity, plummeting to the ground and exploding on impact. Shrapnel flew in every direction. Glass and metal and wire. Grace threw her hand over her mouth, watching the debris blow onto Steph, like hailstones whipping in a tornado.

Thirty seconds passed—or it might have been thirty minutes—before the smoke and rubble cleared. Grace could only look on, shock sitting heavy in her muscles, pinning her to the spot. The explosion still echoed in her ears, droning out the screams of frantic spectators all around her. Her eyes blinked, focusing on Steph's body, willing her to move. To be okay.

The explosion—it was just like in Calvin's drawing. Fireworks shooting off all around Steph's head, threatening to blind her. To burn her. To kill her. But that couldn't be it. Steph couldn't be—

And then she moved, rolling over slowly. She coughed as she sat up, and Grace couldn't believe how relieved she felt. How thankful. Steph was alive. She'd survived the demon's attack.

Grace started to move down the bleachers, but she stopped as she saw Elena, standing there on the court just a few feet away. Elena's gaze was fixated on the floor, on where Calvin's notebook had fallen. On the page open to a drawing of the demon, its lips bloody, its eyes laughing, gleeful.

Would she finally believe now? After the scoreboard had come crashing down?

Grace watched as Elena's eyes remained fixed on the drawing. And then out of nowhere, a breeze cut through the gym, sending chills rolling through Grace's bones. Her nose wrinkled as a sour-sweet smell wafted along with the current, but no one else seemed to notice. The air rustled the notebook pages, and then flipped through them in a flurry. The demon's picture fluttered there on the page for a moment and then began to change in an animated transformation. It morphed into something younger. Something prettier.

Grace gasped as the wind died out and the notebook settled. A smiling face stared back at them. No longer a demon, but a young girl instead.

Something in Elena's face cracked then. Her jaw clenched as she turned to stare down the court at Steph, who was still sitting on the ground, still getting over her near-death experience. A fire filled Elena's eyes and Grace realized what she was seeing.

The girl from Calvin's notebook was there, right in front of them, crouching over Steph, holding her hand and talking to her in a low voice. The likeness was unmistakable.

And as Grace watched her kneel over Steph, checking her arms and face for cuts and bruises, she couldn't help but wonder who exactly this girl was. With a huff, Elena broke Grace's concentration before she stormed off in the opposite direction, leaving Calvin's notebook there on the floor for anyone to see.

Grace scrambled forward then, the shock of the exploding scoreboard wearing off. She bent over and scooped up the notebook, looking back at where Calvin still sat on the bleachers, his gaze transfixed on his trembling hands. He'd need the notebook back eventually, but for now, Grace could hold on to it for him.

CHAPTER 22
ELENA

A hum ran through the locker room as the girls peeled off knee pads, pulled on sweatshirts, and stowed their water bottles. Their eyes couldn't help but dart to the corner, to where Steph was changing. A scoreboard had ripped off the wall and nearly crushed her, and yet she'd shaken off the close call and gotten right back on the court. She'd put up an incredible performance and led the team to a straight-sets victory.

Elena banged her locker open and scowled into its depths. She wished it had been her diving for that ball. Then *she* would have gotten all the glory. Her teammates would be gazing at her with that look of admiration. Steph hadn't even gotten hurt. No broken bones or severed arteries. She'd only gotten a few scrapes and minor burns. And now the whole team thought she was some kind of superhero.

Elena bit her tongue as she watched the girls rally around

Steph, giving her hugs and high fives. It wasn't fair. These girls were supposed to be her friends. They were supposed to be on her side. That they'd turn on her—that they'd believe the rumors flying around school—it made Elena want to kill someone.

But she wasn't a murderer. Henry had said as much in his hospital room. However, that hadn't stopped everyone from whispering behind her back. From spreading the vile lie that she'd pushed her ex-boyfriend into the street on purpose. And now Steph was using this moment of weakness to her advantage. A coup to take over sole captaincy of the team. But Elena wouldn't back down so easily.

Turning back to her locker, Elena tried to look busy. She rummaged around in her bag, keeping an eye on Steph and counting the girls as they filtered out. She was banking on Steph staying back. On being the last to leave. It was the kind of calculated move Elena would pull if she were trying to endear herself to the team.

And as the door swung shut behind Kayleigh, Elena's patience got rewarded. It was just her and Steph left, and Elena wasn't going to waste any time.

Pivoting on her heel, Elena snapped around and slammed her locker shut, pulling out her best snarl as she stalked toward Steph. She had some questions that needed answers, and she wasn't going to put up with Steph's lies anymore.

"Who'd you really see in that mirror?" Elena demanded,

crossing her arms and cocking her hip, readying for a stand-off. "And I know it wasn't Cody Crosby."

This seemed to throw Steph, who fumbled and then acted confused, like she didn't know what Elena was talking about.

"The mirror. Bloody Mary." Elena snapped her fingers with each word. "Who'd you really see?"

"I thought you said you didn't believe in all that," Steph finally muttered, still looking out of sorts.

"I didn't. But now—"

And here, Elena had to think hard. She had to reconsider. The proof was right there in front of her. Nearly impossible to ignore. That scoreboard falling off the wall didn't seem like a random accident. It could have killed Steph.

But Elena didn't want to think about that now. She wasn't ready to believe in demons and curses. And it wasn't important anyway. It wouldn't help her get control of the team back. For that, she needed the truth. She needed to know Steph's secret.

"Who did you see?"

Elena's words cut through the room, sharp and demanding. She moved a couple of steps closer and savored how Steph shrank away, falling even deeper into her corner, her curly hair springing forward to cover most of her face.

"I told you. I saw Cody Crosby."

But Steph's voice wobbled with the lie, losing its conviction.

"You never liked Cody," Elena scoffed, licking her lips. She smirked and caught her reflection in the locker room mirror, her teeth narrowed into fangs. "You've never liked any boy, have you?"

Her words hung in the air. An accusation. Proof. Because—Elena realized with a shock—she'd known this all along.

The way Steph always looked away when the team changed, focusing on the floor or the inside of her locker. The way she'd clammed up at Elena's sleepover the second they'd started talking about boys. All this time, it had been staring her right in the face. The truth. The ammunition she needed to take Steph down for good.

"I'm only going to ask one more time," Elena said, relishing the power, knowing she held all the trump cards. "Who did you see in the mirror?"

A second passed. Then ten. But Elena didn't back down. And eventually, something in Steph broke. Her shoulders slumped and her head dipped all the way to the floor. She wiped at her eyes, sniffling, and Elena knew she had won.

"Fine," Steph whispered, tilting her head back up slowly, her eyes glistening. And Elena almost felt bad for her, for the way she'd secured this victory. It felt dirty. But a win was a win. No matter the tactics.

"So . . ."

Elena watched as Steph struggled with the words, seeming like she'd rather swallow her own tongue than spit them out.

"I saw—I saw a girl. The new girl."

Triumph flooded through Elena, and she almost broke out into a dance right there in the middle of the locker room.

"You happy now?"

Steph's bitterness pulled Elena out of her thoughts. It made her focus on the corner of the room again. There was a fire in Steph's eyes now. A steely resolve as she faced off against Elena, her shoulders thrown back, her chin jutting out, challenging her like they were opponents on the volleyball court. Like she actually had a chance at winning.

"You going to out me to everyone? Let them know I'm a freak? Turn them all against me and get me kicked off the team?"

For once, Elena faltered. She took a step back. That had been her plan, but now—hearing the words from Steph's mouth—it seemed so cruel. So mean. And Henry's words wafted back to her. Was this really who she had become? Did she want to be that girl? She stuttered away from Steph and caught her own reflection in the mirror again. The fangs had retracted, and now she looked kind of lost.

"I don't care that you like girls."

Elena's tone softened, and even though she'd never specifically thought about it, she was relieved to realize it was the truth.

"And don't worry, I'm not going to tell anyone."

"You're not?" Steph didn't seem to believe her. "But what about the team?"

"It's your secret. And they won't care. I'm sure they'd like to meet your new girlfriend."

"Mary and I aren't dating," Steph jumped in quickly to clarify, and the name triggered something in Elena.

"Mary?"

Elena suddenly remembered why she'd wanted to confront Steph. She remembered what she'd seen in Calvin's notebook.

"Yeah," Steph replied, clearly confused.

"You can't date her."

"Why not?" Steph bristled, drawing up to her full height, suddenly ready for a fight.

"Because she's in Calvin's notebook."

"No she's not."

"She is," Elena insisted. "I saw it during the game."

And her confidence seemed to stall Steph, at least for a moment.

"But that doesn't mean anything," Steph countered. "We're all in his notebook."

"It's different with her." Elena didn't know why Steph couldn't see the connection. "It was like a flip book. And Mary—*your* Mary—she transformed. She turned into that—that thing. She became that demon."

"I thought you didn't believe in all that?" Steph scoffed, crossing her arms over her chest as she frowned at Elena. And Elena had to admit, finally, that maybe she did.

"You can't let her get close," Elena pressed. "She's dangerous."

Steph's mouth dropped open, and she spun away from Elena, her hands gripping the edge of the sink.

"Do you know where Mary came from?" Elena peppered Steph with questions. "Or when she even showed up at school?"

"I don't know." Steph shrugged, refusing to make eye contact.

"I thought she was your girlfriend or soulmate or whatever."

"We only just met."

"And you don't think it's weird that her name's Mary?" Elena pressed. "Just like in the game?"

"That's a coincidence," Steph sputtered. "There are tons of Marys out there. It's like the most popular name in the world. It doesn't mean anything."

But Elena wasn't convinced. And Steph didn't seem sure now either.

"I think that she transferred here like two weeks ago." Steph looked like she was thinking hard about it, trying to find the evidence that would disprove Elena's theory. "Yeah. That's it. It was right after you and Henry broke up."

Elena's head ticked to the side, and Steph threw her hands up in defense. But Elena wasn't mad. Something had stuck in her brain. A puzzle piece. But she didn't know exactly how it fit in. Not yet.

"Are you sure about that?"

"Yeah," Steph confirmed nervously. "I remember because I

saw the fight. I mean, practically everyone did. You all had it out right there in the middle of the hallway."

Elena's hand snapped up and Steph fell silent. She needed time to think. To figure this all out. It was right there at the edge of her thoughts. She started pacing back and forth, going over the facts. The dates. Everything that had happened in the past few weeks.

Calvin's visions. Grace's talk of demons. Elena's grandmother's storybook. Steph and her soulmate, who had finally appeared after all these years. Henry's accident. The scoreboard. The mirror. The game. Bloody Mary.

And then it came to her. It suddenly all made sense. She whipped around, but right as she opened her mouth, a crackle ran through the room. The lights flickered and then burnt out completely.

"Steph?" Elena could barely breathe, the darkness creeping in, freaking her out. "Where are you?"

"Here," Steph replied. And Elena hobbled a few steps before finally finding Steph's outstretched fingers with her own, lacing them together and drawing close.

"Did you hear that?" Steph whimpered.

Elena had. And she didn't like the sound of it.

"I think there's someone in here with us," Steph whispered.

"Everyone left," Elena replied, trying to reassure herself as much as her co-captain. "We would have seen them come in."

And just as the words left her mouth, the showers hissed to life.

Both girls startled, though Elena would have liked to believe Steph had jumped higher. She could feel the girl's pulse racing and knew hers was drumming just as fast.

They glanced at each other, their eyes starting to adjust to the dark they'd been plunged into, and made the decision together. They shuffled forward, their hands clasped, knuckles white with fear.

The steam from the shower rose up and hit Elena in the face, seeping into her eyes and nose and mouth. But she pressed on, Steph at her side, walking her right up to the showers to take a look.

And there in the mist, a figure slowly materialized. A chill ran up Elena's spine despite the heat as the shadow took form.

Hair curled out of its head and a long dress fell to sweep the floor. A pair of unblinking, red eyes danced around the room before settling on Elena's face.

A voice then, though the woman hadn't opened her mouth. It echoed through the locker room, low and distorted by the pounding water, impossible to understand.

"What do you want from us?" Elena finally managed to stutter. "Why can't you just leave us alone?"

But the figure didn't seem to hear. Or it didn't care. It kept moving forward, the steam swirling around it, adding volume to its dress and curves to its hips. It floated right up to the girls, and Elena swore she felt its icy breath on her cheek.

I want you.

The words curled through the air, the threat flipping a switch inside Elena, sending her into fight mode.

"You can't have me," she shouted, and her arm flew forward, aiming for the demon's head. But it passed right through, the steam dissipating as a soft cackle bounced off the walls and the showers shut off.

"Did you see that?" Steph asked after a few seconds, her voice wobbling.

"She's not going to win," Elena replied as she stared into the shower, remembering the figure, how confident it had been. How frightening. How in the world were they supposed to beat something like that? Something they couldn't even touch?

She shook her head and turned back around, facing the sinks and the mirror. She gasped, the chill of the moment before freezing her in place. She blinked and took a step closer. But she wasn't seeing things. It was definitely there, written out across the mirror, a finger dragged through the fogged surface.

BLOODY MARY.

The letters were long and unmistakable. A calling card that could not be ignored.

"She's real," Elena whispered, fear prickling the back of her neck. She couldn't deny it any longer.

As she let the truth sink in, the lights suddenly flipped back on, bathing the room in a too-bright brilliance. Elena squinted, trying to adjust, waiting for the spots in her vision to disappear. She rubbed at her eyes and held them closed. But when she opened them again, she wished she'd kept them shut.

Because the message on the mirror was written in bright-red, dripping letters.

CHAPTER 23
CALVIN

White, empty space.

The page stared up at him, a blank canvas asking to be filled. But no matter how hard Calvin tried, nothing would come. Not even the tingle of a vision in his fingertips. A complete block. An artist's nightmare, though he knew better. He'd drawn plenty worse fates over the years. Real nightmares.

Sighing, Calvin let his pen drop to the desk and turned back in his notebook, flipping through until he reached his last drawing, the one from two nights ago, when the scoreboard had come crashing down, nearly crushing Steph. Just like with Henry's accident, Calvin had gone back and filled in the details. The picture hadn't gotten any prettier.

On the gym floor, the scoreboard sparked and sputtered, the wreckage shooting out random electric bolts, firing the last bits of blood from its veins. Smoke spiraled into the air, and in that cloud Calvin could barely make out the outline of a figure, a thing that he knew was no angel.

A knock at the door pulled Calvin out of his daze. Reluctantly, he lifted his head and spotted a familiar face.

"My mom's out in the gym if you're looking for her," Calvin said.

"Actually, I wanted to talk to you," Steph replied, her hands pulling at the strap of her gym bag. "Can I come in?"

"Sure." Calvin quietly closed his notebook and sat up straight, inviting Steph into his mom's office.

Steph hovered in the doorway, rocking back and forth, peeking over her shoulder several times like she was planning on robbing the place, though Calvin didn't think she'd get much for the boxes of old uniforms and sweaty knee pads. Eventually, she must have deemed that the coast was clear because she swung inside and tumbled into the chair opposite Calvin. He could see her eyes roaming, though, traveling over the trophy case behind him, stopping to read every name on every plaque.

"So what's up?" Calvin prompted. They hadn't really spoken since that day at Elena's house, when they'd first tried piecing together all of this Bloody Mary business. Steph still didn't look at him, though. And her gaze had dropped to her lap as she struggled to speak.

"Can I see your notebook?" Steph finally blurted out. And from habit, Calvin's hand pressed down on the leather cover.

But Steph knew his secret. She'd already seen his pictures. It wouldn't hurt to show her now. In fact, it might even help him make some sense of what he'd drawn.

"Fine," Calvin replied, and he slowly opened the pages, letting them flutter underneath his fingertips. "This is from the other night."

Calvin showed her the picture he'd just been staring at, the gym descending into chaos.

"Is that me?" Steph gasped, her finger darting toward the center of the illustration, quivering over the violent details. And Calvin had to remember how jarring it must be for her to see herself in such a dire situation, blood dribbling from the corner of her mouth as sparks shot all around her face.

"It looks worse than it was." Calvin leapt to assure Steph. "Luckily you didn't get seriously hurt. It was a miracle."

"But I thought you drew what was going to happen?"

After she'd been so shy to start, Calvin hadn't expected the question, the curiosity around his talent and curse.

"It's more like—" Calvin tried to think of the right words to explain what he didn't quite understand himself. "A *suggestion* of what might happen. I draw a *possible* future. Usually the worst-case scenario. But they've never come true. Not until—"

Calvin blushed and looked away. He'd only shared this with Grace, but now he knew that, he had to let Steph know, too.

"Not until a few weeks ago, when I drew these."

He flipped through his notebook and pulled out three pieces of paper, the series of visions he'd drawn in the library stacks. He carefully laid them out on his mom's desk so that Steph could see.

"Henry's accident," he explained as he pointed to the picture of Elena with blood splashed across her face. "And now yours."

Steph's eyes grew big as she took in the close-up portrait of her face, the explosions going off around her head like fireworks on the Fourth of July. Her hand strayed to her forehead and Calvin could see her confirming the cut there, in the exact same place as the one on the page.

"Is there something in particular that you're worried about?" Calvin asked, wanting to comfort her. He could tell she hadn't come asking out of curiosity alone. "These are the only drawings you've shown up in. I promise."

"It's not about me."

Steph surprised him with that. And by the way she was chewing on her bottom lip, he could tell she had something big on her mind. So he waited, giving her as much time as she needed, until she finally opened her mouth and spoke, her voice a mouse's peep.

"What about Mary?"

"Who?"

"She's the new girl. Short hair. Always carrying her journal around with her. I think she's in your English class or something. Elena said—she said you'd drawn a picture of her in your notebook, too."

And Calvin realized with a jolt who Steph meant. He remembered drawing her in class on her first day. But that picture—that animation or whatever it was—still didn't make sense to him.

"Do you mean this?"

Calvin flipped through the pages and stopped on the picture of the new girl, a pencil tucked behind her ear, her eyes bright and eager, a dusting of freckles visible across her cheeks.

"That's her," Steph said, looking at the page nervously. "But Elena said that she changed or something."

And Calvin took the pages of his notebook in his hands and flipped through them quickly, watching for Steph's reaction as Mary's face shifted and transformed into that of a demon. He flipped through it a couple more times, before Steph waved him off. They sat there in silence, Steph's eyes glued to the picture, her brow furrowed in concentration.

"What do you think it means?"

And Calvin could tell how much the question meant to her.

"Honestly, I don't know."

Steph fixed him with a confused look. He hated that he didn't have an answer for her.

"Usually my drawings are pretty straightforward. They're disasters. But this—I have no idea what it could mean."

"Could you tell me if she shows up in your drawings again?"

Steph asked, her voice anxious, which made Calvin wonder who exactly this new girl was to Steph and what she was afraid the drawing might mean.

"I'm sure it's nothing," Calvin lied, trying to soothe his own fears as much as Steph's. "But I'll let you know."

"Thanks," Steph said.

And as she got up to go, Calvin was suddenly thankful for the artist's block. He had no desire to see what might come next. No desire to see anyone else's ending.

CHAPTER 24
STEPH

The temperature had dropped, the chill in the air reaching the level where jackets were no longer optional. The local farmers had gotten to work, their harvesters dotting the countryside, cornstalks falling to the onslaught of the machines' gnashing teeth.

In the front seat of her mom's car, Steph was too wrapped up in her own thoughts to notice any of the changes. She couldn't stop thinking about everything that was happening. Everything that felt confusing and so out of her control.

The scoreboard crashing. The message on the locker room mirror. Coming out to Elena. Calvin's drawings. And Steph's feelings for Mary. Mary, who couldn't possibly be the demon. Mary, the girl of her dreams. She didn't want to believe Elena's accusations. She couldn't.

Steph jolted forward in her seat as something prodded her

in the back. She tried to settle back down but the poking persisted until she couldn't take it anymore.

"Stop kicking my seat!" Steph snapped as she whipped around and gave her brother a death glare. His legs twitched, but quit bouncing as he stuck his tongue out at her and turned to stare out the window.

"What's gotten into you?"

Steph did her best to ignore the side look her mother gave her from the driver's seat.

"It's nothing," she mumbled.

"You've been in a mood all weekend," her mom pressed.

"I just haven't been sleeping well."

"Are you having nightmares? Is it the accident?" Steph's mom did her best to keep her eyes on the road despite her concern. "Do you want to talk about it, honey?"

No, Steph didn't want to talk about it. And it wasn't like she could. She could hardly believe the whole Bloody Mary story herself. The second she mentioned that a demon was haunting her, her mom would think she was crazy and probably schedule a meeting with the pastor at their church.

"I'm fine, Mom. Really."

Her mom gave her another sideways glance like she didn't want to drop it, but then cursed under her breath and jerked the steering wheel to the side, almost missing their turn.

"We're here." She tried to play it cool as she came to a stop in the parking lot. In the back seat, Jamie cheered, though Steph couldn't tell if it was from the roller-coaster turn or because they'd arrived.

"Now, your aunt is going to pick you up in a couple of hours," Steph's mom said. "So have your phone on you. And keep an eye out for Jamie. Don't let him wander off."

"Got it, Mom," Steph replied. She didn't love the idea of babysitting her annoying little brother, but she couldn't say no. Not when her mom had picked up an extra shift. Steph's Sunday afternoon was a minor sacrifice. So she pushed her shoulder into the car door and stepped outside, standing next to Jamie, who had already clambered out.

"And try to have some fun," her mom called, leaning into the passenger's seat to get a better look at her kids. "Everything's going to be okay. I promise."

This last bit was clearly meant for Steph, and she tried to believe it as she shut the car door, waving goodbye as her mom headed out.

"All right, Jamie." Steph turned to give her brother the ground rules, but he'd already taken off, making a beeline for a group of kids gathered around a picnic table over by the barn doors. Steph could only sigh and start after him.

As she walked, the wind blew past her and through the trees overhead. The branches shivered from the cold, creaking as they did their best to hold on to their last leaves. And so did Steph, the air racing underneath her jacket, chilling her to the bone. She squeezed her arms against her body and tried to keep every bit of warmth she had as she approached the group of kids buzzing ahead of her, their talk filled with excitement for hayrides and pumpkin picking. Running through the corn maze. Getting their faces painted with bats and skeletons and ghosts. Halloween was only a week away, and the pumpkin patch had kicked things into high gear.

A few of the parents nodded as Steph joined the cluster of nine-year-old boys. She'd chaperoned Jamie at enough of these birthday parties for them to recognize her, even though none of them ever really tried talking to her. Which was fine. She didn't know what to say to a bunch of middle-aged moms anyway. And she had plenty on her mind already. Starting with Elena.

The girl knew her secret.

Why hadn't Steph lied? It would have been so easy to deny it. But a part of her felt relief in that confession. In finally saying those words out loud. It was the first time she'd admitted that she liked girls. That she was gay. It felt good, even left her a bit giddy.

But what about Mary?

Steph couldn't help but feel sick thinking about Calvin's notebook. The pictures of Mary transforming into the demon. It didn't make any sense. She couldn't have fallen for a demon, could she? Mary wasn't this malignant spirit haunting them. Which made Steph wonder—

What did the demon want?

To kill them, obviously. It'd already come for both Elena

and Steph. And Calvin's drawings made it clear that it had plans for Grace as well. But was there something else it needed from them?

If only Steph knew German. Then she could read that storybook and maybe make some sense out of all this. But as it was, she didn't have a clue. She was defenseless. Which terrified her. It was like going up against an opponent on the court without having scouted them. Without a game plan. If they picked the wrong strategy, they wouldn't stand a chance.

A shiver ran up Steph's spine and she blinked, coming out of her thoughts and suddenly realizing she didn't know where she was. Stalks of corn a couple of heads taller than her crowded in on both sides. But luckily, she spotted the rest of the group up ahead. She hurried to catch them, chastising herself for spacing out. She didn't even remember walking into the corn maze. There was no way she'd be able to find her way out on her own.

When she got to the kids and moms, her eyes swung around the group, looking for her little brother. She did a double take, counting them off this time, panic fluttering in her chest. Because Jamie wasn't there.

"Have you seen my brother?" Steph asked, but the closest mom only shook her head.

"He came in here with us," another offered. "I'm sure he just fell behind. Don't worry. He'll find us. It's not like there's a real monster out in the maze."

And the rest of the women chuckled. But not Steph. With

her heart hammering, she whirled around and headed back the way she thought they'd come. Because she knew that there was a monster out there.

She turned left and then right, navigating down the narrow rows, the corn brushing up against her shoulders, making her jump.

"Jamie," she called, ignoring the fake spiders and cobwebs she passed. The sheets draped over poles, holes cut out of their heads to make them look like ghosts. "Jamie! Are you there? Where'd you run off to?"

This way. He's over here.

Steph heard the whispers and veered after them. But then she stopped, realizing that they weren't her friend. She flipped on her heel and set off in the opposite direction, doing her best to ignore the voices.

He's over there.

Trust me.

You'll never find him on your own.

But Steph shook her head and kept calling.

"Just come out and I promise I won't tell Mom."

Still no response. So Steph picked up her pace, practically flying through the maze, having no clue where she was going or if she'd already come this way. She could be running in circles for all she knew. And the whole time, she couldn't help imagining the worst.

Stumbling across her brother lying unconscious on the

ground, blood oozing from a set of claw marks in his back. Or she'd find him strung up in the corn, his face frozen in horror, there to scare off the crows.

She pushed herself on, the cornstalks blurring into an unbroken wall, hemming her in, squeezing her tight, narrowing into a line until she couldn't breathe or move or see or think.

She turned a corner and stumbled into a clearing, her knees hitting the ground as she tripped. Her hands pressed against the cold earth.

He's right here.

The whispers surrounded her, coming out of the corn from all sides.

You found him. Look up.

And slowly, Steph complied, her head lifting, her eyes rising. And there, right in front of her, the demon stood, its tattered gown whipping in the wind, its grin a wicked and wide thing. It hovered two feet off the ground. A harpy. Ready to swoop down and snap Steph up in its talons.

Steph scrambled back, dirt digging under her nails. She wanted to look away, but her head wouldn't turn. Her eyes wouldn't blink. She wanted to scream, but she couldn't make a sound. Instead, she retracted as far as she could until her back was pinned against the stalks of corn.

What's the matter? Not who you were looking for?

Steph gritted her teeth and tried to make the voice go away. Tried to find the energy to flee. To get the heck out of there.

It's too late. Come with me. We'll find your brother together. I promise it won't hurt.

Steph blinked and the demon closed the distance in a flash, an inch from Steph's face, its icy, rough hand grabbing her chin. The tips of its nails hooked in her skin, pinning her in place. Steph couldn't move. Couldn't push away as the demon's foul breath filled her lungs. Its bloodshot eyes searched her face and its free hand slid up to her forehead, tracing the cut the scoreboard had left, pressing it open again as Steph cried out.

You think you can escape your fate?

The voice cackled in Steph's head even though the demon's lips hadn't moved.

Save yourself the pain. You can't win.

And for a second, Steph believed it. She imagined how much easier it would be to give in. To slip away right there in the cornfield. To leave it all behind—the fight with Elena, her annoying little brother, her loneliness, the fact that she would never fit in, her feelings for Mary.

No. Not Mary. She couldn't give her up. Not after she'd spent five years searching for her. Five years figuring out who she was.

You can't protect her.

Steph's muscles fired, and she pushed herself to her feet, throwing the demon off her. Then she bolted away, back into the corn maze, hazarding one last glance over her shoulder, not looking where she was going until she abruptly plowed into someone.

"Whoa! Are you okay? What's got you in such a hurry?"

Steph whirled around at the familiar voice, relieved that she wasn't alone and then suddenly terrified as she recognized the girl.

"You look like you saw a ghost," Mary said.

She tried to catch her breath. Tried to make sense of what had just happened. Of what was happening now.

Did demons make jokes? Did their eyes crinkle like that when they laughed? Steph didn't know what to think. She wanted to believe in Mary. To believe in her soulmate. But how could she be certain?

As the questions ran through Steph's head, Mary stepped past her, a curious angle to her chin, and made her way toward the opening Steph had just barely escaped.

"No, don't go back there. There's a—"

But Steph cut off her warning as Mary turned to face her, a look of confusion wrinkling her brow.

"What? The scarecrow?"

Steph's eyes darted over, and she couldn't believe it. Where the demon had been standing only a moment ago there was just a straw-stuffed scarecrow. And it wasn't even a scary-looking one.

"Are you trying to prank me or something?"

Mary pulled Steph's attention as she rejoined her.

"No. I didn't—" Steph sputtered, unsure, the demon still burned into the backs of her eyelids.

"Are you okay?" Mary sounded concerned. Her fingers flew

to Steph's forehead and Steph pulled back instinctively, remembering the demon's cold touch. "You're bleeding."

Steph touched the cut and pulled her hand away, inspecting her sticky red fingertips.

"I'm fine." She wiped away the trickle of blood with her sleeve, but then remembered why she was out here. "Have you seen a nine-year-old boy? About this tall? It's my little brother. I think he's lost and I don't know where—"

Steph had lost her breath again and felt like she was going to pass out. She could run volleyball drills for days, and yet right now she could barely stand up straight. Her hair was a mess. Sweat beaded her forehead. Her hands were covered in dirt and blood. She'd probably never looked worse. But she didn't care because she was so worried.

"Calm down. It's going to be all right."

And Mary's hands landed on Steph's shoulders, grounding her, pulling her back from the worst-case scenarios running through her head.

Demons couldn't do that. They couldn't calm Steph down. They couldn't make her stomach flutter.

"I'm sure he found his way out," Mary said calmly. "We can head to the front and let the staff know. I think they have a drone or something they can use if he's lost out here."

Steph stood there for a moment, torn, but Mary's plan made sense. Wandering around the maze blindly hadn't helped her find him.

"Thanks," Steph mumbled. "Can you lead the way? I got kind of turned around."

Mary nodded and took off, Steph falling in line one step behind her, doing her best to discreetly untangle her curls and wipe the sweat and blood off her face. She rubbed her palms against her pants and hoped that got rid of most of the dirt, but she could still feel it under her nails.

"Wait, what are you doing here?" Steph asked, catching up to the girl.

"You mean here at the pumpkin patch? Or like, what am I doing as a person on this planet?"

"I mean the pumpkin patch." Steph did her best to stifle a laugh. A joke. Another check in the not-a-demon column.

"I thought it'd be nice to get out. Maybe find a story worth writing about. And I was dying for some fresh air and exercise."

"Did you ride your bike here?" Steph remembered their first meeting at school, watching Mary pedal away.

"I ride my bike everywhere."

"But we're pretty far out. Why didn't your mom or dad drive you?"

"It's just me and my mom," Mary replied. "And she was busy. Always working on her latest scheme to take over the world."

Steph paused at that, and her expression must have dipped. Demons had plans for world domination, didn't they?

"Relax." Mary smiled and pulled Steph along. "She's not like a supervillain or anything. She's a real estate broker."

They kept walking, Steph unsure of what to say, her mind still on her missing brother. And still trying to puzzle out who Mary really was. Demon or soulmate?

But standing next to the girl, Steph had a hard time seeing anything bad in her. She was so light and cheerful. She was helping her out. That was definitely not something an evil spirit would do.

"So what's with this Harvest Halloween Carnival thing?" Mary asked. "I keep seeing all the flyers at school."

"Oh, that? It's like this big fundraiser they put on each year. Costume contests and bobbing for apples and tons of food and rides. The whole town comes out. But the first night is just for the high schoolers."

"It starts on Wednesday, right?"

"Yeah. And then ends on Halloween on Saturday."

"Ta-da," Mary exclaimed, and Steph lifted her head to find that they'd arrived back at the entrance to the corn maze.

"That was fast."

"I'm a good navigator. Now, do you see your brother anywhere?"

Steph scanned the distance and immediately spotted the other kids and moms poking through the pumpkin patch, picking out their jack-o'-lanterns-to-be. And right there in their midst was her little brother.

"Jamie," she shouted, relief washing over her and then quickly getting replaced by anger. His head picked up at the sound of his name and his eyes went big as Steph twitched her thumb for him to come over. He looked scared as he slunk toward her, keeping his eyes to the ground, and she hoped he'd remember that next time he decided to run off.

"Do you not remember what Mom said? No going off on your own."

"I told you I had to pee," Jamie pleaded his case. "You said it was all right as long as I hurried back."

And the bad thing was that Steph couldn't remember if she had said that or not. She'd been so wrapped up in her own thoughts in that corn maze.

"Well, no more disappearing." Steph put her foot down, her anger subsiding some. "You've got to keep me and the rest of the parents in your sights at all times."

"Fine," Jamie grumbled, digging his toe into the ground. And then he ran off to the rejoin the kids.

"Thanks for the assist," Steph said, turning back to Mary, feeling her cheeks and ears redden now that it was the two of them alone again.

"So, are you going to be at the carnival?" Mary asked. "It'd be nice to have someone to show me around."

And as Steph's heart raced in her chest, she nodded. Because demons didn't flirt. And they definitely didn't ask girls out.

CHAPTER 25
ELENA

Elena didn't have much of an appetite as she pushed her food around her plate, her silverware clanking against the china, filling the silence in the dining room. Who could eat when there was a demon on the loose? A demon set on killing her?

"How's Steph doing?" Elena's mom asked, stirring Elena from her thoughts. "The poor thing must be frightened to death after the game the other night. What a freak accident."

"She's fine," Elena mumbled before turning back to her plate, where she was drawing crop circles in the fluffy mounds of mashed potatoes. She also wanted to say that it hadn't been an accident, but she knew her mom wouldn't believe her. No sane person would.

"You know, I'm really proud of how well you've been doing with the team," Elena's mom pushed on, and Elena could tell she was trying to throw her a bone. "And your dad's proud, too. It takes a lot of commitment to lead."

"To co-lead," Elena corrected her, not wanting to think about her dad, who hadn't been to a single game all season. Who was too busy with business trips to show up.

"Well, either way, it's hard work and a big responsibility."

Elena shrugged, and a quiet settled around the table again, thoughts of a rampaging demon filling Elena's mind until she couldn't take it anymore.

"Mom, did Grandma ever seem—" Elena struggled to find the right word. "Disturbed?"

"Do you mean Grandma Whittaker?"

"No, I mean Dad's mom."

Elena's mom nodded as she set her fork down and thought about it.

"Your grandma Meyer was always a quiet woman. But she loved you. She had a hard life, moving over here from Germany all by herself. Raising your father in a new country."

"Did she ever seem scared? Like she was running from something? Or hiding?"

A beat passed between them, Elena's mother looking at her strangely.

"What's got you so interested in your grandmother all of a sudden?"

Elena worried that she'd said too much. "Just curious, I guess. I was up in her room the other day looking through some of her old stuff."

"You should ask your dad when he gets back. He can go through her things with you."

Elena didn't have time to wait for him, but she smiled nonetheless, nodding at her mother as if she were going to take the suggestion.

"I have a quiz to study for."

"Study hard," her mom replied, and Elena backed away from the table, feeling guilty as she left her mom alone in the dining room. But she had more important things to do. A demon to stop, if she could only figure out how.

Climbing the stairs, Elena couldn't help thinking about that message on the locker room mirror. The threat in those blood-stained letters.

Time was running out. The demon was coming after them. Getting stronger. There was no telling what it'd do next. Who it'd try to hurt. She had to stop it. So she headed to the only place where she might find answers.

Sliding into the bedroom, Elena left the door open a crack behind her but didn't flip on the light. She didn't want her mom to come poking around. And if she squinted, she could see well enough from the streetlights outside. Elena moved to the bed and bent over, reaching under the mattress to haul out a large cardboard box. She sat down on the floor and opened the lid, diving inside her grandmother's remaining keepsakes.

First, she pulled out a stack of old black-and-white photographs, people who Elena didn't recognize except for her grandmother, looking young and elegant, a version of herself that Elena had never known, though she could see the family resemblance, the similarities when she looked in the mirror at herself. In each photo her grandmother wore the same necklace, the thin chain glinting around her neck. Seeing it, Elena could remember playing with it when she was little. Tugging at it as her grandmother read to her. She would have liked to wear it, but she had no idea where it had gone. Probably lost somewhere in her grandmother's room. Or maybe she'd been buried with it.

Elena set the photos aside and pulled out a box of letters next, all of them written in German. She didn't even bother going through these, knowing that she wouldn't be able to make any sense of them. She kept rifling through the box and pulled out the book of fairy tales. The family heirloom. A treasure. She sat back on the floor, crossed her legs, and set the book in her lap.

She flipped through the pages slowly, scanning them for clues. Circled passages or words written in the margins. She didn't find anything out of the ordinary, though, so she turned to the story.

"Die Verflucht Frau."

The Cursed Woman.

Wasn't that what Grace had looked up on her phone?

Elena's eyes flickered to the shrouded mirror in the corner, making sure it hadn't moved closer, hadn't come unsheathed. She didn't want anything to do with it. She didn't even like being in the same room with it. She could feel its energy seeping into the space. Dark and disastrous. Trying to draw her in.

Come and take a closer look. See how beautiful you are.

She shook her head and got back to the story, focusing on the words, sounding them out the best she could, hoping that something would jump-start her memory. She could try to translate it herself, but that would take weeks, and she didn't have the time or the patience.

So instead, she stared at the page and tried to remember. She tried to hear her grandmother's voice reading to her. Her grandmother who would visit a couple of times each year, her hair a snowy drift on top of her head, piled this way and that depending on which way the wind blew. She'd died over five years ago, while Elena had been away at volleyball camp. Elena hadn't even gotten the chance to say a last goodbye.

Frustration burned through her, flushing her cheeks and scorching her fingertips, causing her to drop the book. Why had she come in here? She couldn't make sense out of the story. It was all so useless.

She picked the book back up and stared at the cover, running her palm over the embossed leather. And then, out of nowhere, a shock tingled through her hand. A memory jumped up and possessed her.

She was sitting with her grandmother, playing with that necklace while the woman held the book of fairy tales open on her lap, pointing at the pictures as she tried to get Elena's attention.

The memory started to fade, but Elena tried to hold on. To concentrate on that scene. What was her grandmother trying to tell her? To show her?

Elena closed her eyes and she was back there, only seven or eight years old, with an attention span of two seconds. She didn't care about the story, but then her grandmother pulled out a long leather bookmark. She waved it in front of Elena's face. Then she tucked it into the back of the book and whispered a *poof* as the bookmark disappeared.

Elena pawed at the book, riffling through the pages in search of the missing placeholder. But it had vanished. A magic trick. And Elena clapped her hands in amazement, demanding the secret to the trick as the bookmark reappeared between her grandmother's fingers, as if she'd pulled it from thin air.

This time, her grandmother showed her. She pointed out the tiny slit hidden in the back cover. A secret compartment that only they knew about.

Elena stared at the book in front of her, the memory flickering out as suddenly as it had come on. Her finger trembled as she slid it along the top of the back cover, her nail snagging on the tiny slit, invisible to the eye. She dipped into the secret compartment, pulling out the same bookmark from her memory and an envelope with her name written on the front.

She swallowed as she took in her grandmother's sweeping scrawl, afraid of what the letter might hold. But this was what she'd come looking for—a potential explanation. Hands unsteady, Elena broke the envelope's seal and pulled out the letter. She had to stop several times as she read, puzzled but also scared by the words within.

Dearest Elena,

I fear that I might not make it to your sixteenth birthday. And for that, I am sorry. At this point, I imagine you've begun to hear her. You're still too young to pass this burden to, but I've felt her at my back the last few months, nipping at my heels. She's slept for so many decades, gathering strength, and I'm afraid that I won't be able to keep her at bay for much longer. I'm trying, but if you're reading this, then I failed.

There's a secret that the women of our family have passed down for generations. A task that you must take up when I am gone. Not all fairy tales are make-believe. Remember the stories I've told you. I hope they have prepared you for what's to come.

The mirror should have been passed to you in my will. Find it. Watch over it. Keep it safe. She's trapped inside it, but that doesn't mean she's powerless. She still has her charms and tricks. Do your best to resist them. Don't fall for her lies. Keep her locked away.

And if she does get out, you must put her back. The mirror holds the key. Use it. The demon will want *revenge for what we've done, and I don't want you to pay that awful price.*

Stay safe. Stay vigilant. And know that I love you.

Her grandmother's signature took up the last lines of the letter, a flourish of ink that matched the body's frenzied, cursive scrawl, as if her grandmother had been racing the clock to finish. Elena reread the note, looking for more details but not finding them.

More confused than ever, she got to her feet and peered across the room, fixing her eyes on the covered mirror. She took a step forward. And then another. She had to urge her legs to move each time. When she got to the mirror she stood there for a few seconds, taking in deep breaths. Then she reached out and tugged the sheet to the side.

The mirror stared back at her, its face unchanged. Still ruined. The gash zigzagged across the glass like a lightning bolt. And the gaping crater in the middle was all the proof that Elena needed.

With a sinking feeling, she realized that she'd already fallen for the demon's tricks that her grandmother's note had referenced. It had already escaped. And now she had to figure out how to put it back. Or else.

The mirror was the key.

It was what her grandmother had written. But how?

Against her better judgment, Elena leaned forward, practically pressing her nose up against the broken glass. She ran her fingers over the inset pearls. Felt the grooves of the script running around the frame.

The script.

She squinted and tried to make out the words carved into the old wood. It wasn't in any language she recognized, but she still tried sounding out the letters, mouthing them the best she could.

She'd gotten a quarter of the way around the mirror when her phone vibrated in her pocket. She ignored it, continuing with the script. But her phone buzzed again and then a third time, insisting she answer.

She pulled it out and saw that a string of messages had come in from her anonymous admirer. Their texts had slowed down over the past week, and Elena had honestly begun to lose interest. What did she need with a digital boyfriend? Especially when she still didn't know who he was. She moved to put her phone back in her pocket, but it shook again as another message came through.

We should meet.

And then a couple of seconds later, another buzz.

At the Halloween Carnival.

That got Elena's attention. He wanted to meet her. In person. Finally. Tomorrow night.

It almost made her forget about her grandmother's note.

She hovered there for a moment, glancing between her phone and the mirror. She knew she needed to figure this out first, so she leaned in close again to finish reading the filigreed script.

But as she concentrated, a fog seeped into her brain. Cold fingers crept across her chest and moved up around her neck. Her head grew light, her breathing shallowed, her eyes closed halfway as she pressed to finish. But the words sounded all wrong coming out of her mouth, and she felt so stupid.

This was useless. What was she even doing? She didn't know anything about demons or spells. She had no idea how she was going to lock this thing back in the mirror.

But you do know how to flirt with boys.

She did.

And don't you deserve to have a little fun?

Turning back to her phone, Elena hesitated for a moment and then typed out a reply. As she waited for an answer, she bent down and picked up the sheet, tossing it over the mirror, making sure it was fully covered.

She hadn't forgotten about the demon, but it could wait one more day. She could figure this out after the carnival.

As another message pinged into her phone, Elena turned her back on the mirror. Warm air filled her lungs again as she walked out of the room, her mind working on another problem— trying to figure out what killer costume she should wear when she finally met her anonymous admirer.

CHAPTER 26
GRACE

Where was he?

Grace stood just inside the entrance to the Harvest Halloween Carnival, hands worrying away in their long white gloves. She rose to her tiptoes and tried to see through the crowd.

He must have had second thoughts. It shouldn't have taken this long. He must have abandoned her when he'd gone to buy the tickets. It was the story of her life. And after everything had gone so well earlier that night with her dad. Calvin had showed up on time—fifteen minutes early, even—and played nice all evening. He'd smiled and posed for pictures, given all the right answers and asked a few questions of his own. He'd put on the costume Grace had picked out without a single complaint. And he'd taken the face paint and worked his magic on them both. They looked ten times better now. They were sure to win the couples contest.

So why had he decided to bail now?

She'd scared him off. She'd come on too strong. She should have known it was too good to be true. The matching costumes. She shouldn't have made them bride and groom. He must have read into it.

Or maybe he was mad at her for dragging him here. For wasting precious time. They should be researching how to stop the curse. Grace should be trying to save him. Every second mattered.

But hadn't Calvin insisted they take a break? Hadn't he made her put down the grimoire that had finally arrived that morning? He'd wanted a distraction. He'd wanted things to feel normal for once.

And then, right as Grace's panic grew unbearable, he appeared, his green head sticking out from everyone else as he lumbered in his square-toed shoes, his knees stiff and his arms held out straight in front of him for full effect.

"Hope I didn't keep you waiting too long," Calvin said as he approached. "That line took forever. But I got them."

A string of red tickets fluttered from his hand and Grace couldn't keep herself from hopping up and down in excitement, her worries disappearing like a banished poltergeist.

"Where to first?"

"Well, there's the Headless Horseman," Grace said as she reached up and snagged a stream of tickets. She pointed out the Tilt-A-Whirl that was painted black and orange with fiery pumpkins flying across it and a mounted, decapitated Hessian in pursuit.

"And then the helter skelter."

They walked past the Beetlejuice-colored turret that was poking out of the ground, a pair of riders screaming as they careened down the spiral slide attached to the structure's walls. Out of the corner of her eye, Grace noticed Calvin's cheeks turning even greener than his face paint, and she could have kicked herself. These rides must all look like death traps to him.

"But we can skip those." Grace quickly changed course. "There's plenty of other things I want to do. Like skele-dogs!"

She pulled him over to the nearest food stall and pointed out the corn dogs. There was a ketchup skull piped on the outside of each. She held up two fingers and the concessions worker handed them to her.

"I don't know why, but it just tastes better at the carnival." She took a bite and hoped she hadn't gotten ketchup all over her chin, though the bloody effect might add something to her costume.

"So what made you pick these outfits?" Calvin asked after three bites, finishing off his skele-dog in record time.

Grace took a few moments to chew, hoping she wouldn't say the wrong thing. But he already knew she was a monster movie nerd, didn't he? She swallowed and wiped her mouth with a napkin.

"I wanted to do something classic. And there aren't that many female characters in the monster movie universe. So

Frankenstein's monster and his bride were kind of a perfect fit. Do you like it?"

She winced, hoping he would, but also knowing that he'd tell her he did even if he didn't.

"They're awesome!" Calvin cheered, and she could tell he wasn't lying. "I don't think I've ever looked better."

"You have," Grace assured him, giggling. "And your paint job took it to the next level."

She batted her lashes and showed off her face. He'd managed to make her look like the most glamorous reanimated corpse ever. Sunken eyes and hollow cheekbones. But like a model for some avant-garde photo shoot. It was kind of incredible what he could do.

"We're going to kill it in the couples costume contest," Grace said. "That is, if you still want to enter."

"Of course we're entering," Calvin exclaimed. "And we're gonna win."

Grace's heart fluttered. Why did she keep underestimating him? And herself? She had to quit that.

Careful. The closer you get, the more it will hurt when he's gone.

Grace gulped at the thought. Remembering that Calvin only had so much time left.

"Should we hit a ride before my shift?" Calvin asked. "I've got about thirty minutes before I'm scheduled to take over the booth."

Calvin had taken Grace's advice and signed up with the art club. He'd already drawn several monster portraits that would be auctioned off throughout the week, so he didn't have to worry about what visions might come to him in the moment.

"Are you worried at all? That something might happen?"

Grace hated that she had to ask. But she knew that his visions could come on at any time. And she knew how bad it got when they took over.

"I'll be fine," Calvin assured her.

But that didn't stop Grace's anxiety.

"We should be figuring out how to break this curse," Grace said, feeling silly now for agreeing to come to the carnival in the first place. "We should be trying to save you. We don't have time to waste. Look, I brought the grimoire with me."

She'd showed him the spell book at her house, but he'd made her promise not to bring it. Promise to keep the night normal. No talk of demons. But she just knew that she'd find the secret in the grimoire's pages. She'd come across a lost language or a sealing ritual or something. The solution.

"We can look at it later," Calvin said softly, his hand wrapping around Grace's wrist, his grip gentle yet firm.

"But what if there isn't a later?" Grace blurted out, her worry racing ahead of her.

"It can wait," Calvin said, and his lips settled into a heartbreaking frown, leaving Grace speechless.

"Look, I have time for one ride before my shift," Calvin explained. "So let's go on a ride. Just pick something relatively safe."

Grace grew flustered. She didn't agree with Calvin, but this was what he wanted. To be normal for at least a few minutes. And she could look through the book while he worked his shift. Then she might have something concrete to show him after he finished.

"We can try Bats in the Belfry," Grace suggested.

And she took his hand and led him through the carnival, weaving between stalls and avoiding the largest clusters of people. They passed witches and ghosts and princes and princesses. Vampires and pirates. Everything under the moon, both costumed-out and costumed-lazy.

"It's the spinning cups," Calvin realized as they came up to the ride.

"Think you can handle that?"

Calvin nodded, letting Grace tug him into the relatively short line.

Again, the ride was Halloweened out, each cup painted black, with wings and white fangs thrown on for effect. Even so, it would have had a hard time scaring a third grader. Grace knew it had to be the safest ride at the whole carnival, and she patted herself on the back for thinking of it. After a couple of minutes of waiting, they handed over their tickets and climbed into one of the bats by themselves.

As the ride started up, Grace twisted the turntable in the center of their car and the world started spinning around them. Slowly, at first. But then they gathered speed, the lights of the carnival streaking to a blur around them, the wind whipping them in the face as they twirled, sliding across the seats, colliding into each other.

With each bump, a thrill ran through Grace. She could hear Calvin laughing next to her, his face bright, and she realized she'd never seen him like this. So free. So happy. And she wanted to open her mouth to tell him what she suspected he already knew. That she liked him. That she *still* liked him. That she liked him so much it hurt. That worrying about him kept her up at night.

She had to tell him. Tonight. She couldn't wait any longer.

But as the ride slowed and the world stilled around them, Grace's courage abandoned her. The words stuck in the back of her throat.

"I better head over," Calvin said, his arm stretched out to help her up.

Grace blinked and tried to shake herself out of her stupor. Then she took his hand and climbed from the spinning bat, stumbling as she found her footing back on solid ground.

"Don't worry, I'm not going to abandon you before the big contest," Calvin went on. "I'll find you when I'm done and we can head over together."

His smile told her that he meant it. And it was exactly why she liked him so much. He just got her. He always knew what to say. He cared. She'd tell him how she felt later. And in the meantime, she had some homework to do with the grimoire.

CHAPTER 27
STEPH

Steph couldn't believe that she was here. Here at the carnival, eating out of a bag of creepy crawlies. Here watching Mary pick through the popcorn kernels in the trail mix to unearth the gummy worms buried deep.

Here *with* Mary. The two of them together on what probably wasn't a date but felt like one nonetheless based on how Steph's stomach rolled with nerves, how she worried about saying and doing and liking the wrong things. This was her chance, and she was so afraid that she would mess it up.

"I love all the spooky names they came up with," Mary said, bringing Steph out of her spiraling thoughts. "It really gets you in the mood, doesn't it?"

Steph watched as the girl raised a gummy worm to her mouth and bit it in half, a wicked delight spilling over her face as she chewed and swallowed.

"The mood?"

"Halloween," Mary exclaimed like it was obvious. "Ghosts and goblins. Things that go bump in the night. It's all so spooky and thrilling."

"Oh, right." Steph nodded, though her recent experience had taught her the opposite. The problem with scary was that usually it came with a reason to be afraid.

"And I love getting to dress up," Mary went on. "You get to be whoever you want, even if it's just for a few hours. It's the only night of the year we all get to play make-believe. We all get to write whatever stories we want to live."

Steph looked down at her costume, the athletic shorts and knee pads she'd thrown on. Her hair pulled up into a ponytail. The jersey covering her chest.

She'd gone as what she already was. A volleyball player. And now she realized how stupid it must look—basic next to Mary's scaly face, which must have taken her hours to draw on. Her hair was tinged green and wrapped in coils, each with a head sprouting out of the end, pairs of black eyes and hissing tongues probing the air, looking for a victim. A modern-day Medusa.

"I don't know," Steph said, swallowing an M&M. "Isn't Halloween all about nightmares? I mean, who wants those to come to life?"

"One person's nightmare is another person's adventure."

Again, Steph would have disagreed, but she didn't want to come off as a wimp. So she smiled through the uneasiness bubbling in her stomach and nodded along.

"Should we hop on a ride?" Mary asked, her focus leaping ahead so easily, making Steph wish she wasn't so stuck in her head. So afraid of messing things up.

But a ride was something she could do. Something she liked. The thrill was kind of like what she felt on the volleyball court. Adrenaline pumping through her body, making her strong and confident. Unstoppable. Which was something she could really use right now.

"That one looks fun."

And Steph's eyes darted ahead to see which ride Mary had picked out.

"Witches Take Flight." Steph read off the ride's name, thankful it wasn't the Ferris wheel. She wasn't ready for something like that. Not yet, at least.

"See, that's exactly what I'm talking about," Mary chirped as she hurried Steph along, pulling her into the line. "That kinda name puts you in the Halloween spirit. Way more than calling it the swing ride."

"I guess," Steph admitted.

And this time the smile that bubbled to her lips was natural. Real.

"So, is it everything you hoped it would be?" Steph asked as they waited, blushing when Mary turned her full attention on her, her stare almost turning Steph to stone. "I mean the carnival . . ."

"It's better," Mary said. "The carnival and my guide. I'm glad I convinced you to show me around."

And then Mary hit her with that smile, sweet and big and white, the corners of her eyes crinkling adorably. Irresistible. The face she'd fallen for in all her dreams. Not the face of a demon at all.

What had Steph been thinking? She didn't know how to do this. She had no clue how to tell this girl that she liked her. How to figure out if Mary might like her back. Did she need to come out to her first? Or find out if Mary even liked girls like that?

"Make sure you hold on tight."

Steph blinked, thinking she'd heard wrong. Then she realized it was their turn on the ride.

"Sit close to me."

As if Steph needed the invitation. She hurried to beat the rest of the riders and strapped herself into a chair right next to Mary. She wrapped her hands around the swing's cold chains and looked across at the girl next to her. Her feet were already dangling off the ground, her tiptoes skimming the dirt as the carnival workers checked everyone's harnesses. Mary looked back at Steph and gave her a thumbs-up, causing Steph's stomach to flip before the ride had even started. An alarm bell rang and the chains clanked to life. The swings rose up off the ground, slowly. They started to spin. And then they were flying.

Steph felt like she was caught in a tornado, the wind whipping her around in a circle as she hung on for dear life. Her legs flew into the night sky and the centripetal force pressed her up into the air. A scream leapt out of Steph, and she could see Mary returning the call, the glee ripped from both of their mouths. Steph had never felt this light. This free. Like anything was possible. She wanted to hold on to that sensation. She wanted to defy gravity for as long as she could.

Up here she didn't have to think about demons trying to kill her or her classmates finding out she was gay. She didn't have to worry that Elena would turn the volleyball team against her. Steph could leave all of those worries behind and just enjoy the moment. Enjoy the high—

A loud clank rang through the air.

The ride shuddered suddenly, throwing everyone to one side. The swings lurched with an unimaginable violence, and all of a sudden, Steph really was hanging on for dear life.

The vibration shook through the chains. Through Steph's fingers and up her arms.

She lost her grip as the swing juddered right and then left, sending them all careening toward one another, inches from a midair collision. Steph heard Mary's shriek and tried to reach her. Tried to pull her close, keep her safe. But the swings wouldn't let her.

They were going to die. They were careening at sixty miles an hour. Out of control. Their swings were going to detach, cannonballs flying out over the carnival to wreak even more damage.

And then, mercifully, the ride began to slow. The swings dipped and dove in crazy curlicues, but none of the chains snapped or threw their riders in the air. The machinery righted itself and ground to a halt, its passengers breathing hard, tears on most of their faces. A few knuckles flashed red as people grappled to get loose. One person moaned on the ground, gripping an ankle. And another must have hit their head on one of the chains, as blood dripped down into their eye. The ride attendant hurried over to call for a medic, but Steph had stopped paying attention. She fumbled to unfasten her harness and leapt out of the seat, rushing to Mary, pulling her close in one sweep of her long arms.

"Are you okay?" Steph whispered into the girl's reptilian tendrils. "Are you hurt?"

The girl quivered in Steph's grip, tears spotting her cheeks, smearing her carefully drawn-on scales. But Steph didn't see any cuts or broken bones. There weren't any outward signs of trauma.

"You're okay. We've got our feet back on solid ground."

Steph repeated the mantra, hoping it'd soothe Mary, even out her ragged breaths.

"I'm here. Nothing bad is going to happen to you. We're safe now."

Steph hoped that Mary believed it. Because she certainly didn't.

"*You.*"

The word skewered the air, an accusation lodging in Steph's back, right between her vertebrae as she recognized Elena's voice. She hadn't realized she was on the ride.

"I'll be back in just a second," Steph said, because Mary didn't need to hear this.

She marched over to head Elena off before she came any closer.

"We could have been killed," Elena whisper-shouted as she stepped out of her own harness, her face bright red, her poufy hair a vulture's nest on top of her head. The neck of her dress fell off one shoulder, the costume now more countryside maid than French royal. She leaned to one side and shot a glance in Mary's direction, but she didn't go after her.

She was afraid, Steph realized. A feeling she hadn't even known Elena could have.

"She didn't have anything to do with this," Steph snapped.

"Are you blind?" Elena had lowered her voice to a seething whisper. "She showed up the day after I broke the mirror. She's Bloody Mary in the flesh. What more proof do you need? She's the one causing all of this."

"She's not—" Steph hiccuped, taken aback. Surprised even though she knew she shouldn't have been.

"Did you talk to Calvin?" Elena demanded. "Did you see his drawings? The way she transforms? If you weren't so head over heels you might have noticed the signs. You might have realized that she's the enemy."

"Mary's not a demon."

Steph didn't think she'd ever spoken so forcefully in her life. But Elena refused to back down. The two co-captains just stared at each other, a stand-off to end all stand-offs, until Elena finally broke.

"If you don't do something about her, then I will."

Elena's words vibrated in the air.

"Don't you dare."

And Steph let her own threat sink in before blinking away from the staring contest, turning to look for Mary.

"I warned you," Elena called after her. But Steph ignored her. She kept her focus on finding Mary and on the fact that they'd survived another close call that night. They'd gotten lucky. Again.

"There you are," Steph said, jogging to catch up to Mary. "Let's get out of here."

And as they walked away, Steph wrapped her arm around the girl's shoulders to keep her close and comforted. But she couldn't shake the morbid thought. Couldn't help wondering what would happen when her luck finally ran out.

CHAPTER 28
ELENA

She'd almost died. Almost crashed and burned right there on that overgrown swing set, a tragedy the news would have called a freak accident, even though Elena knew better. Knew that there were other forces at play.

But Elena had held on tight. She could still feel the cold chains pressing into her palms, how they'd almost cut into her skin. She hadn't let the demon toss her into the night sky like a rag doll. She'd won. And now, standing across from the ride, watching the carnival workers rope it off and post an OUT OF ORDER sign out front, she realized that she wasn't afraid. Not anymore. All the close calls had only made her skin thicker, steeled her against fear of the end, prepared her to take on a demon, to carry on her grandmother's legacy.

Her head flicked to where Steph and Mary had disappeared.

That demon.

Elena was sure of it now. She should go after them. She could put a stop to all of this right now. And she would have, except—she didn't know how.

The mirror holds the key.

Elena remembered her grandmother's words but still hadn't figured them out. She didn't know how to put the demon back, what would happen if she tried and failed. Would it even work now that the mirror was broken? Was she already too late?

Frustration burned through Elena. Her brow furrowed as she stewed. She hated not having the answer. She hated being stuck. But what could she do? She needed more time to figure it out, to go through her grandmother's things again to see if she'd left any more clues. She needed to reexamine the mirror. Maybe there was another secret compartment hidden in the back. Or maybe it was like a magic mirror and she could just wish the demon away. She didn't think it'd be that easy, but there was always a chance. It had worked in other fairy tales.

Elena's head hurt from thinking so hard and getting absolutely nowhere. She wasn't going to solve this tonight. She'd just have to wait until the morning and keep her guard up in the meantime, steering clear of that girl and Steph, which wouldn't be too hard since they appeared to be together.

And then the thought struck her. Had Steph and Mary been on a date?

No. That wasn't possible. Steph wasn't even out yet. She wouldn't. She couldn't. Not when Elena herself was still single. Still waiting on her mysterious texter to show his face.

She fished in her purse and pulled out her phone. The screen flickered and she stared at it, willing a text to come through. He was supposed to message her. They were supposed to meet. Finally. Tonight. But she hadn't heard from him all day. Was he ghosting her?

No. There was still plenty of time. She was going to meet him and find out exactly which upperclassman was hiding behind that set of perfect abs. She was going to have a hot new boyfriend, and then she wouldn't be the dateless one.

As the phone screen went dark, Elena's reflection flashed in the glossy black rectangle. She could have screamed. She looked terrible. Her makeup smeared. Her hair a tangled mess. Her tiara sitting crooked, barely hanging on to her head. That ride had done a number on her. She couldn't risk meeting her future boyfriend looking like this. She had to fix it. Now.

She scurried across the carnival grounds, her head held low, hand up to cover her face the best she could. Spotting a bathroom, she ducked inside, thankful it wasn't a porta potty.

Staring into the mirror, Elena realized the damage was worse than she'd thought. She looked like a monster, the zombie of Marie Antoinette who'd had her head sewn back on. It was all wrong. Luckily she'd brought her supplies. It'd been a chore to lug them around all night, but now it was paying off. She tipped her purse over and her makeup spilled across the counter. She picked up the eyeliner and got to work.

As she redrew her eyes, added highlighter to her cheeks, and powdered her nose, Elena got lost in the routine, in the magic, as her blemishes disappeared, her skin smoothed, and she painted over her imperfections. A calm fell over her, almost like a trance, hypnotized by her own reflection.

That's right. Make yourself beautiful. Make yourself irresistible.

Elena finished with her face and moved on to her hair, watching the locks fall against her shoulders as she pulled it down. She ran a brush through the tangles. Unkinked the snags. Then she swept it all back into an updo, hitting it with hair spray, teasing it out to make it big and beautiful and luxurious.

Magnificent.

Then Elena picked up a tube of lip liner. She twisted the top off and marveled at the deep red color, leaning close to the mirror, tilting her chin up. Carefully, she drew the brush across her throat, filling in the scar, the guillotine's bite.

I can make you a queen. Everyone will bow before you.

She stared at her reflection, her nose pressed close to the glass, as if she planned on climbing through the mirror.

I can give you everything you ever wanted.

Elena's pink lips smacked as she examined her face. Her perfect, beautiful face. She didn't think she'd ever looked better.

All you have to do is ask.

A part of Elena knew the compliments were false. She knew that the demon was trying to trick her, like her grandmother had warned. But it was hard to resist the attention, to see through the flattery. There was something powerful in the praise. Something irresistible.

Her phone buzzed, and Elena's eyes flitted down to the screen, then back up to her face.

One last look. For confidence.

She swept all of her makeup into her purse and headed out, floating through the maze of carnival booths and rides, on her way to finally meet her dream boy.

She passed ghost hunter dart games and bat ring tosses. Water gun wars where jack-o'-lantern balloons swelled to ginormous size before bursting. She dipped between bubbling cauldrons of cider and farm stands of candied apples. And then she spotted it. The Haunted Hall of History, a museum of silly made-up artifacts. The attraction where her mystery boy had told her to meet him. Only, no one was there.

Elena sidled up to the front doors, glancing at her phone to make sure she hadn't mistaken the message. She hadn't. So she waited, watching people pass by, her heart quickening when someone appeared but then flatlining again when they passed her by. What was taking him so long? She didn't have all night to wait.

"Elena?"

She jumped when she heard her name and spun around. She hadn't even seen him come up. Then the door to the museum banged closed and she realized he must have been inside, waiting for her. Watching her.

"Are you—"

Elena cut off as she realized she didn't know his name. Didn't have anything to call him.

"I am," he replied, tipping his black, brimmed hat, which was pulled low over his forehead.

He was shorter than she'd imagined. And a mask covered the majority of his face so that Elena couldn't tell who he was. But as long as he had that six-pack hidden somewhere underneath his costume, Elena didn't mind.

"For you, my princess," the boy said with a flourish, and Elena had to laugh as a rose appeared between his fingers. With the cheesy trick and his cape fluttering behind him, he looked kind of like a kid magician. But the Z on his chest gave his costume away.

"Zorro?" Elena asked, taking the rose and delicately pressing it to her lips, hoping it made her look mature.

"At your service." He took her hand and kissed it, which sent butterflies dancing in Elena's stomach. Something about his voice sounded familiar, but even as Elena looked close, she couldn't figure it out.

"So are you going to take off that mask and show me who you really are?" Elena asked, doing her best to sound sultry.

"I've been dying to find out. And then maybe I can give you a real kiss."

The Zorro jerked back, his fingers picking at the hem of his cape. The bottom third of his face that Elena could see tightened, his lips pursing into a nervous seam.

"Here, I'll help you." Elena leaned forward, leaving only a couple of inches between them. Her arms flowed around the back of his head, undoing the bow that kept his mask in place.

"Fine," the boy said, his hands snaking around her wrists. Hands that seemed too small and delicate for a junior or senior. "But promise you won't be mad."

Elena didn't have time to think about that as she lowered the mask and revealed her admirer's face—a face that she suddenly, infuriatingly, recognized.

"Martin," she screamed as she pushed him away, her body shaking, her head on fire.

"You said you wouldn't be mad," the boy whimpered.

"Have you been texting me this whole time?" Elena sputtered, the fantasy crashing down around her. "Did you steal my number from your brother's phone?"

Martin shrank away, looking like the twelve-year-old he was, his mom catching him with his hand in the cookie jar. He was the kid brother Elena had witnessed annoying Henry for the last three years. The one Henry had told her had a crush on her. It seemed cute back then. But now—now it was just gross.

Elena couldn't believe it. He had fooled her. She had been

texting with a seventh grader for almost a month. *Flirting* with him.

"You—you—liar."

And before she knew it, her hand flew out and smacked him across the face.

Tears welled up in his eyes. But she knew it couldn't have hurt that much. Besides, he was the one in the wrong. He was the one who had tricked her. She was the victim here. She deserved to be angry. Deserved—

She couldn't look at him anymore. She had never been so embarrassed. She had to get out of there. Had to make sure no one saw. That no one knew. She spun on her heel and took off, making it all of five steps before spotting Grace.

"Are you okay?" Grace asked, stopping Elena's angry march. She was standing there with Calvin, both of them sporting big blue ribbons pinned to their chests. The happy costume-contest-winning couple. She could tell they'd been having a good night by their smiles. By the way they leaned into each other.

"I'm fine," Elena snapped, even though she was nothing of the sort.

"Is that Henry's little brother?" Grace asked, pointing over Elena's shoulder. "Is he crying?"

Elena sneaked a glance back to where Martin had dissolved into a pile of tears and snot.

"What'd you do to him?"

"What'd *I* do?" Elena huffed. It was the wrong thing to ask.

Anger boiled right underneath her skin, scalding her insides as it bubbled. She couldn't hold it back. "*He* catfished me. *He* tricked me into flirting with him."

"Wait," Grace interrupted her, and Elena saw recognition twinkle in the girl's eyes. She realized it was too late. "*He* was the guy you were texting with? *He's* the reason Henry broke up with you?"

"It's none of your business why we broke up," Elena shouted, happy when Grace took a step back. Happy to see the girl fishing out a necklace from underneath her dress, nervously fingering the charm. A locket that suddenly looked all too familiar.

"That's not yours."

Elena couldn't believe it. How could Grace possibly have it? She took two steps forward and snatched the necklace out of the girl's trembling fingers. Her grandmother's necklace.

"Hey," Calvin cried. "That was Grace's mother's!"

"No, it's not." Elena tugged the locket closer, dragging Grace's head down with it. "It's mine. My grandmother left it to me."

"Give it back." Calvin looked ready to fight, which Elena found both surprising and pathetic. Did he like Grace that much? "It's all Grace has left of her mother. She gave it to her before she died."

"Before she died?" The question popped out of Elena's mouth even though it wasn't a question at all. Her eyes met

Grace's. Saw the silent plea. And she knew. Elena wasn't the only one who'd been lied to.

"Grace's mother isn't dead." Elena spoke the words carefully, relishing every one of them. She wanted to make sure Calvin understood.

"Yes, she is," Calvin replied, as if he were some sort of expert in the subject. "She died in a car wreck. You were there. You heard. We waited for her dad to come pick her up."

Elena tsked, shaking her head. What had this girl gotten herself into?

"Her mom didn't die." Elena drew out the words like it was obvious. "She broke her collarbone. And then she left. She lives in Ohio."

"No. That can't—that can't be true."

Calvin had turned to Grace, disbelief causing his voice to waver. But Elena didn't give Grace the chance to explain. What did she care about Calvin's feelings?

"When did you take this?" Elena dangled the necklace in front of Grace's nose, demanding an answer.

"It was an accident," Grace sputtered, and Elena couldn't tell if she was explaining it to her or Calvin. "I didn't mean to—"

"When?" Elena cut her off. And Grace seemed to break in two, her shoulders collapsing as she curled in on herself.

"That day we were in your grandmother's room. When my mom had her accident."

She'd had it for five years? And pretended it was her mother's all that time? Elena's lips curled into a snarl.

"How pathetic."

Elena turned to go.

"Pathetic? You want to talk about pathetic?"

Elena whipped back around. Was Grace really talking back to her? She'd never snapped at her like this.

"At least I haven't been flirting with a seventh grader."

Elena opened her mouth, but before she could get a word out, Grace launched a second attack.

"And for the record, I'm the one who told Henry about your text messages. I snuck into the locker room and stole your phone while you were practicing. I'm the one who outed you as a cheater."

Elena jerked back, her mouth falling open in shock. Grace had told on her? Grace had ruined everything?

"And you know what?" Grace barreled on. "I'd do it again. Because you're mean, Elena. You're a bully. You don't deserve a boyfriend like Henry. And you never deserved a best friend like me. You deserve to be lonely and miserable."

Rage coursed through Elena. An intense fury ten times worse than she'd ever felt. Her cheeks glowed red. They burned in the night, like Grace had slapped her across the face.

"At least I'm not a thief," Elena shot back. But even that wasn't enough. She needed to drive the dagger home. She needed to bury Grace. "At least my mom didn't leave me."

She knew she'd gone too far the second the words passed her lips. But it was too late to take them back. Too late to do anything but watch Grace's face crumble. Watch tears spring to her eyes. Watch her turn and bolt into the night, her sobs echoing in her wake.

"You're a bully," Calvin muttered before taking off after Grace. And Elena suddenly realized that he was right. She was.

CHAPTER 29
CALVIN

Where had she run off to?

Calvin's eyes swept along the carnival aisles, looking for that white-lightning-streaked cylinder of hair. It shouldn't be that hard to find a Bride of Frankenstein. *His* Bride of Frankenstein. They'd won the couples costume contest together, and now he felt suddenly incomplete without her.

Did he care that she'd lied to him? Yeah. It bummed him out that she hadn't been honest. That she didn't think she could trust him, especially after he'd opened up to her about his drawings and the visions. But that was also what made it hard to stay mad at her.

She'd listened to him. She'd understood. She hadn't laughed or called him crazy. She'd actually believed him, something he didn't think anyone ever would do. And now she was trying to save him. He couldn't give up on her. At least not without giving her a chance to explain herself.

Moving through the crowd, Calvin's head swiveled around like a periscope, hunting but not finding her anywhere. He couldn't give up, though. He'd just have to keep searching until—

A flash of light in Calvin's peripheral vision caught his eye. Immediately, he flipped his gaze around and spotted the building, its lights flickering as another bulb exploded with a sizzle and pop.

THE DEVIL'S FUN HOUSE.

Calvin shivered as he read the illuminated words. But something in him knew it was a sign. He knew he'd find Grace inside. Despite his better judgment, he made a beeline for the attraction. He ignored the BACK IN TEN MINUTES note stuck out front and eased the door open, letting himself be swallowed whole by the devil's red, grinning mouth.

"Grace," Calvin called quietly, squinting to see through the dimly lit room, through the fog rising up from the floor in chalky clouds. "Are you in here?"

He waded in deeper, coughing as he inhaled some of the fog, gagging at the ashy, brimstone smell. He held his hands up in front of him to make sure he didn't run headlong into anything solid and tried his best to ignore the flames climbing up the walls, casting the whole room in a hellish red light.

"Grace, you can come out. You can talk to me. I'm not mad. I promise."

Calvin took another couple of steps and froze as his reflection suddenly appeared twenty times in front of him, echoing off the fun-house mirrors. He looked tall and stout and willowy and

239

buff all at the same time. And when he called Grace's name again, his mouth went big, devouring his whole face, while in another mirror it shrank down, disappearing altogether into his neck.

"Grace," he called again, but his voice came out smaller this time, the sound devoured by the jumping flames.

His breathing grew heavier and his legs wobbled underneath him as his eyes darted from mirror to mirror, traveling over all of the distorted faces, not recognizing himself in any of them. Losing his grip on reality as he forgot who exactly he was.

Was he sad Calvin? Grinning Calvin? Surprised? Angry? Scared? Betrayed? Laughing? Heartbroken?

His pulse jumped as his gaze fell on one reflection in particular.

Do you see?

Calvin wished he could unsee it. He hadn't forgotten that fourth picture he'd drawn in the library. The one he hadn't shown to anyone.

Is it how you always imagined it?

Calvin's fingers inched along the lines of the reflection, tracing the curve of his cheek, drawing his eyes rolled up into his head. His mouth hanging open. His lips lax. His face void of any emotion at all. His skin pale. Cold to the touch.

Your end is coming no matter how hard you try to ignore it.

Calvin jumped as something skittered behind him. He whipped around and thought he saw it. Someone running, darting across the mirrors just out of reach. In and out. Over

240

and through. He ran after it, making his way deeper into the maze, following the sounds because he couldn't trust his eyes.

He weaved through the dozens of versions of himself, his breath growing short, his heart pounding in his ears. He raced through the fun house, trying to keep up. Trying to get ahead. He chased until he ran right into a dead end.

His fist pounded against the mirror, the glass shaking as it held firm. He exhaled and a puff of frozen crystals colored the air. His nostrils twitched as something foul ran under his nose. Grace could be anywhere. He'd never find her.

Then he heard it. A quiet sob. But he wasn't going to be fooled. Not again. He closed his eyes and rested his head against the cold glass. However, the noise persisted. He wasn't imagining it. This time, it was real.

He turned and followed the sound, navigating through the maze carefully this time, his fingers skimming the glass, keeping him on the right track. He moved out of his dead end and into an open space he had missed the first time through. And there she was, sitting on the ground in a crumpled pile, her shoulders pulsing up and down as she cried.

"Grace?"

She lifted her head and looked up at him. Her tears had washed streaks of gray paint from her cheeks, and her eyes were red and swollen, shot through with pain.

"You found me," she whimpered, so low that Calvin could barely hear. "I didn't think you'd—"

But more sobs bubbled out of her.

"Grace," Calvin said again as he bent down on his knees so that he could look her in the eyes. "It's okay."

She sniffled and swiped at the tears, smearing her face paint more, staining the fingers of her gloves.

"I'm sorry I lied to you. It's just—sometimes it's easier to think of her as dead. It's easier than the truth."

"The truth?" Calvin sat down in front of her, pulling Grace's hands into his and squeezing them. He listened to her breaths. Waited for her to be ready.

"She left us," Grace whispered, tears edging her voice. Only this time she managed to keep them from falling. "After the accident. She said it was a wake-up call. She could've died, and what had she done with her life?"

Grace hiccuped then, her lips curling into a pained smile, trying to brush it all off.

"She wasn't happy. We didn't make her happy. So she left. She abandoned us. She abandoned me. Just like Elena did when we were best friends. Just like you're about to do now that you found out I've been lying."

She dropped her head again and turned away.

"I'm not going anywhere," Calvin whispered, his hand sneaking underneath her chin, gently pulling her eyes up to meet his. "I'm your soulmate, aren't I? It's fate."

And as their gazes held for five and then ten seconds, something in Grace relaxed and a smile slowly blossomed on her lips.

A real, heartfelt one, more beautiful than any Calvin could have drawn.

"Thank you."

Then she hugged him, her face pressed into his shoulder, his shirt soaking up the last of her tears. When she pulled away, there was a new light in her eyes. An excitement in her voice.

"I think I found something," she whispered, and then dug into her purse, pulling out the book of spells.

"You were looking through this while you were hiding?" Calvin couldn't believe it.

"I said I'd find a way to save you. I couldn't give up on you. Not even if you never wanted to talk to me again."

"Grace." Calvin shook his head, marveling as she rushed to show him what she'd found.

"Look, there's a whole chapter in here about mirrors. About how they can be used for scrying or as portals. How they can be opened and sealed shut for good."

She flipped through the book and showed Calvin.

"Somehow," she went on, "we must have opened a portal five years ago. And if we want to get rid of this curse—this demon—we have to close it back up again."

Calvin didn't know what to say as Grace looked to him expectantly. He wanted to be as excited as her. As hopeful. But—

"How do we even do that?" Calvin asked. And Grace frowned, her brow wrinkling in on itself.

"I'm not exactly sure. But I think it has something to do with that inscription. The words running all around the mirror's face. If I can just decipher it, then I might be able to break the curse."

"Oh." Calvin didn't know why he sounded so disappointed. What had he really expected? Some magical cure? He'd stopped believing in that a long time ago.

"But I'm still going through the book," Grace hurried to add. "I just know I'm going to find it. Something I can use to translate it and get the right pronunciation."

You'll never get rid of me.

And in the mirror, Calvin saw it, floating there in front of them, its hair swirling around its head, a look of wicked triumph stretching its lips into a grin.

Your end is coming, and there's nothing you can do about it.

A cackle echoed through the fun house, its shrill pitch shaking the mirrors so that Calvin thought they might all break. Beside him, Grace could hear it, too.

"We have to get out of here," Calvin shouted, and grabbed her hand, pulling her into the maze, too afraid to look back. They stumbled through the rows of mirrors, losing their balance over and over again, nearly falling flat on their faces.

"The book," Grace shouted, and Calvin wheeled around, realizing she'd dropped it. "We can't leave without it."

And even though he could see the demon flying behind them, flitting from mirror to mirror, Calvin took off, running back into danger. He was already going to die, so what did he really have to lose?

He saw her swooping down, going for the book. But he couldn't let her get it. At the last second, he dropped to his knees, sliding forward, his hands reaching, grabbing the book seconds before the demon could, his momentum carrying him forward as his foot collided with the mirror. A splinter shot up the glass, cracking it into a hundred pieces, and a horrific scream cut through the air, rattling every mirror in the fun house, shaking them until—

"Duck!" Calvin shouted, doing his best to get up. He lunged for Grace, his arms outstretched to cover her, but it was too late.

With a sickening crunch, every mirror in the fun house exploded, knocking Calvin and Grace off their feet, shooting thousands of shards of glass into the air in a glittering cloud of shrapnel.

A ringing filled Calvin's ears as he staggered to his knees, shaking pulverized glass from his shoulders and hair.

"Grace? Where are you?"

He shuffled forward, squinting through the dark room. Glass tinkled around his feet, the sharp edges scratching at the ground.

"Talk to me, Grace. Tell me you're all right. I can't lose you."

And then, just as the panic was taking over, he heard a cough. He saw something moving in the shadows.

"I'm here," Grace called, and Calvin ran to her, relief

breaking over him. He dropped the spell book and flung his bag on the ground, pulling her close as he checked on her. She had a long cut running up her arm, but it seemed shallow. It would be okay.

"I was so worried," Calvin exhaled.

But the shell-shocked Grace didn't seem to hear him. She could only stare into the empty space, her mouth moving even though no words came out.

"It was my drawing," Grace finally murmured. But Calvin didn't know what she meant. He hadn't drawn this. Not like the scoreboard. He hadn't seen it coming.

"Your premonition," Grace explained. "The shards of glass."

And then, before Calvin could stop her, she reached into his bag and pulled out his notebook. She flipped through the pages and grabbed the series of drawings he had shown her in her bedroom.

"See?" Grace pointed at the glass, the hundreds of shards that Calvin had drawn surrounding her face. "Elena. Steph. And now me. They've all come true."

But as Grace flipped through the pictures, she froze. Her jaw dropped as her eyes scanned the page. As she realized there had been a fourth drawing in the series that Calvin hadn't told her about.

"Calvin."

It was all he needed to hear to know the truth. But still, he reached out to her, his hand trembling.

"It's not what you think."

"Why didn't you show me this?" Grace asked, her brow furrowing, confusion clouding her eyes.

And Calvin couldn't look at her. Couldn't take the guilt. So he turned and stared at the page instead. Took in the details. His own body laid out on the ground, cuts open across his face, blood spotting the front of his shirt.

And the worst part—that Grace was there, too. Weeping over him. Cradling him in her arms as she sobbed. Crying over his lifeless body.

"Why didn't you tell me that I'm with you when you die?"

"It's not—" Calvin began, but Grace had already gotten to her feet. The drawings dropped from her trembling fingers, and she bent over. But she scooped up the grimoire instead, holding it close to her chest, like it might be able to shield her from another attack. Or maybe from Calvin.

"I can't be with you," Grace mumbled, still in shock.

"Grace, listen to me," Calvin pleaded. "It's just a picture."

"No," she insisted, starting for the door, blood beginning to trickle down her arm. "You have to stay away from me."

Calvin reached for her. He tried to convince her to stay. He didn't care about the drawing. He'd grown tired of running from his fate.

"I said, stay away from me!" Grace screamed, shocking Calvin, freezing him in his tracks. "I won't let you die."

And then she was gone.

CHAPTER 30
GRACE

The halls were empty when Grace poked her head out of the girls' bathroom, which meant she'd succeeded in avoiding a certain somebody, as the entire student body had rushed home to start the weekend after the final bell had rung. And as a bonus, she'd nearly finished the grimoire translation, though it hadn't been a very easy project to work on while tucked away in a bathroom stall, her notebook balanced on one knee while the spell book sat precariously open on the other.

She riffled through the pages of notes she'd made, mouthing the pronunciation guide she'd cobbled together. The grimoire had held the secret after all. And after two days of focused study, she thought she'd cracked the incantation from the mirror. She thought that maybe she could save Calvin.

That was why she'd pushed herself. Why she'd stayed up until she fell asleep at her desk with her cheek pressed against the spell book. Why she'd ignored his texts and avoided him in the hallways. Why she couldn't see him. Not if she wanted him to stay alive.

That picture told the future. She was there when he died. She cradled his head in her lap. She heard the last breaths whisper past his lips. She felt his skin grow cold as his heart stopped beating. She was the last thing he saw, so why had he spent so much time with her? Why had he sought her out? Why had he lived so dangerously?

Grace shook her head, trying to get rid of the nightmare. It was like she'd already lived it even though it hadn't happened yet. Even though it wasn't going to happen. She would break this curse. Calvin wasn't going to die. He couldn't, as long as she didn't see him.

Out of habit, her hand swiped up to her neck, but it only grabbed air. As if she could have forgotten that Elena had taken the locket at the carnival. Taken back what Grace had stolen in the first place.

Grace had to remind herself of that. The locket had never been hers. The woman in it wasn't her mother. She could never fill that hole.

But all of that didn't matter now. She had to focus on stopping the demon, shutting it away forever. It was October thirtieth—the eve of All Hallows Eve. And something told her that she had to end this curse now. Tonight.

"Grace?"

She jumped at the sound of her name, and her notebook and the grimoire went flying, landing on the floor with two thuds.

"Sorry, I didn't mean to scare you."

But Grace backed away from the apology. She ignored the outstretched hand that had retrieved her things off the floor.

"I've actually been looking for you."

"Don't you have practice or something?" Grace asked, not knowing what else to say.

"Coach won't mind if I'm a few minutes late," Elena replied, biting her bottom lip. Which made Grace pause. Made her marvel. She'd never seen Elena unsure like this. She'd never seen her not demanding control. Even when they were little and still best friends, Elena had always been the one to lead. She'd never deferred to anyone.

"Look, I'm sorry," Elena eventually squeaked, and Grace had to lean in really close to make sure she hadn't misheard. "For the other night. At the carnival. I went too far when I brought your mom up like that. It was a low blow. I shouldn't have—"

She petered off then, and her hand crept its way up to her neck, pulling on a familiar silver chain. The locket, Grace realized with a start. It'd already found a new home.

"The truth is, I really need your help," Elena went on, filling up Grace's silence. "And I know you kind of hate me, but you're the only one who has a shot at figuring this curse out. You and that monster-obsessed brain of yours."

She'd tried to make it sound flattering, smiling at the end—a compliment, even though Grace knew that if Elena had said it a few days ago, it would have been the opposite.

"So I'm asking you for help," Elena added, stumbling to fill the void. "I'm begging for it, really. I can't do this by myself."

Grace had never felt so powerful. And she had to wonder that she'd never thought to use this tactic before. Silence to make her voice heard. To force Elena to show her hand.

"Please," Elena pleaded. And it was clear she was losing her patience. She'd come to the end of asking nicely. "Do it for Calvin."

This finally broke through Grace's resolve. The last thing she wanted to do was help Elena, but she didn't really have a choice.

"I'll help you," Grace muttered. "But only because I need to save him."

She reached out and took the notebook and grimoire from Elena.

"Thank you, thank you, thank you," Elena trilled before snapping into motion. She swung her backpack off her shoulders and dug around in it. "I found this hidden in the book of fairy tales. My grandmother knew about the demon. Guarding it is like a family legacy or something."

She held an envelope out, and Grace took it, unsure of what she'd find inside. But as she skimmed the handwritten lines, understanding began to settle over her. The demon wasn't anything new. It had been trapped for centuries, waiting for someone as pliable as a bunch of kids to awaken it. They'd unwittingly done just that when they'd played that game all those years ago. They'd brought this on themselves, and now they were the only ones who could put it back.

"The mirror holds the key." Grace read the words out loud, thinking.

"I know," Elena babbled. "But I've checked. There aren't any secret compartments in the back. There isn't a hidden lever or anything."

"It must mean the inscription," Grace said, her brain racing ahead of her words, piecing it all together. "The incantation circling the mirror."

"But that's all nonsense. It doesn't even use real letters. How are we supposed to read that?"

Grace's eyes lit up. This was the reinforcement she'd needed. Now she knew she was right.

"I found a way to translate it." Grace held up her notebook, tapping the sheet, showing Elena her hard work. "It's all right here."

Elena eyed the page skeptically, the phonics-like way Grace had written out the pronunciation guide.

"But this doesn't even make sense." Elena scoffed and rolled her eyes. "It's all gibberish. What are we supposed to do with it?"

"I think . . ." Grace furrowed her brow. She didn't know exactly how to do it, but she'd read through enough of the grimoire to get a basic understanding of how most spells worked.

"I think that as long as I'm there with the mirror and reciting the spell, then I can close the portal and seal the demon inside."

"So we can lock it away for good?" Elena asked. "Simple as that?"

"Well . . ." Grace thought about it some more. "The demon might put up a fight. It probably won't like that we're trying to seal it away. But I think there are some ways we can strengthen the spell. Some precautions we can take."

She thought about what she'd read in the grimoire. About salt circles and burning incense. About lit candles, amulets, and other protections. In theory, those should all work for this ritual, too.

"And we could do it tonight?" Elena sounded eager, which was a good thing. At least for Calvin's sake.

"Yeah," Grace replied. "I think I can get everything ready. It might take a few hours, though."

"That's fine. We can meet at my house. Put an end to this demon for good."

Grace nodded, liking how sure Elena sounded, needing to latch onto that certainty.

Tonight. They'd lock the demon away. They'd stop the curse before it could catch up to Calvin. They'd save him.

"But promise you won't tell anyone," Grace hurried to add. "Especially not Calvin. He can't know. He can't be a part of this. He can't be there."

"Fine with me."

Elena didn't ask any questions. Which was good. Grace didn't want to have to explain. She couldn't. She choked up every time she thought about it.

"Meet at my house at seven," Elena said. "Tell your dad it's a sleepover if you have to. Don't be late."

And before Grace could get in another word, Elena turned and jogged away, slipping into the gym. Grace stared at the doors as they swung shut, thinking about all she had to do. Thinking about what would happen if she'd translated the spell wrong. If it didn't work.

But it had to. They didn't have any time to lose.

A locker banged and Grace blinked. She turned her head and her pulse jumped into her throat.

Calvin.

Their eyes met across the lobby, and Grace felt a tug in her gut. Was it attraction trying to bring them together? Or Calvin's fate?

He looked like a corpse already, with large purple bags under each eye and his hair sticking up in every direction. She wanted to go to him. To make sure he was all right. But she knew she couldn't. So she spun on her heel, racing out the school doors without even one glance back.

But tomorrow. Tomorrow this would all be over. Tomorrow she could see him again.

CHAPTER 31
STEPH

Exhaustion settled over Steph's bones as she walked out of the gym. But it wasn't just from the hard practice. She'd been living with one eye open for the past two days, worried about what might come next. Who might get hurt.

Steph's gaze fluttered back into the gym, and something twisted in her gut. The fallen scoreboard had been cleaned up and the hardwood polished so that it looked good as new, like nothing had gone wrong.

But that uneasy feeling stuck with her. Like the second after a fuse sparked or a weapon was drawn. The first moment after a car skidded out of control on a rain-swept highway. That palpable fear of knowing something was about to happen. Something terrible.

Henry. The scoreboard. The carnival ride. It wasn't over yet.

There was still something out there hunting her. And Steph

knew it wouldn't go away on its own. It would find her. It would find her friends. Her family. And then it'd hurt them. Unless she could figure out a way to stop it.

Steph's focus wavered as a movement in the gym caught her eye. Her gaze flickered to the side and she spotted a familiar face rounding the corner.

Mary. An unexpected but welcome sight. Steph's heart jumped, but then came crashing right back down, missing the easy put-away kill.

Because Mary was talking to Elena. Elena, who hated her. Who thought the girl was a demon. Whatever they were talking about, it couldn't be good. Steph's shoulders tightened and she started back inside, but before she'd gotten through the door, the other girls shook hands and parted ways. Elena noticed Steph and gave her a hard stare before turning and walking out a different exit. Mary, on the other hand, came bounding over.

"What'd she want?" Steph asked, pointing to where Elena had disappeared. "I can talk to her. She shouldn't be bothering you."

"Bothering me?" Mary's chin tilted and Steph realized that she really hadn't heard what had gone down at the carnival.

"Just be careful around her," Steph said uneasily. "She's not your friend."

"Why? Because you and I have been hanging out?"

"I don't know. Maybe?"

Steph thought about it, but figured she'd leave it at that. It wasn't like she could just come out and tell Mary that Elena thought she was a demon that they'd accidentally released from an old mirror.

"Well, you don't need to worry. She was only helping me with my story."

"Your story?"

"For the school paper," Mary said, a grin lighting up her face. "You're looking at their newest reporter."

"That's great. So what's your first big scoop?"

"Well, it's you."

"Me?" Steph didn't quite believe it.

"You and the rest of the team," Mary admitted. "But you'll be a big part of it. How you and Elena are sharing the captain responsibilities. How you two have led the team to a winning season. I was hoping that you'd let me interview you. Figure out what makes you tick. We've hung out a few times, but there's still so much I don't know."

"All you have to do is ask."

Steph heard herself saying the words and couldn't quite believe they'd come out of her mouth. She wasn't exactly an open book. There were some things she couldn't say. Things she still didn't understand. Things that Elena better have kept her mouth shut about.

"Do you have a few minutes now?" Mary asked, getting her journal out and pulling her signature pencil from behind her ear.

"Sure. What do you want to know?"

"Let's start with, how did you get into volleyball in the first place?"

And as Steph began telling her story, she found that the words slipped right out of her, flowing more freely the more she talked.

She told Mary about joining her first volleyball team and learning the game. About getting the MVP award at her first club tournament. About how she'd found her footing on the court. How she'd learned to embrace her gangly arms and legs, her height that put her a head taller than almost every girl in their grade. How she was hoping they could win the district tournament next week. Hoping she could get good enough to earn a scholarship to play in college so her mom wouldn't have to worry about loans.

The details spilled out of her, and when she'd finished answering all of Mary's questions, Steph found that she wanted to say more.

"Can I tell you something else?" Steph asked. "Off the record?"

"Sure," Mary replied, leaning close as she shut her journal. "What's on your mind?"

"I think—"

And Steph knew she was acting crazy. Knew she was being too spontaneous. It was too early to say anything. Especially to Mary. But she trusted her. She could tell her anything. And weren't they meant to be?

"I think I like girls."

A pause stretched between them, and Steph wondered if she could take it back. If she could retract the statement and pretend like it'd never crossed her lips.

"You think?" Mary lifted an eyebrow.

"I know." Steph blushed, and her eyes dropped to the floor, staring at the white, scuffed tiles. "I know I like girls."

And it felt so weird to say it like that. To be so sure. But she was. And she was ready for a friend to know.

"Well, is there any girl in particular?" Mary nudged Steph with her toe, but Steph didn't look up. She couldn't without giving herself away.

"Maybe," she mumbled. She wanted Mary to know that she was gay, but she wasn't ready to admit her crush just yet. She wouldn't be able to bear the disappointment of a rejection.

"You should tell her."

Mary nudged her again, and this time Steph raised her head, saw the warm smile on Mary's face, radiating that positive energy. And Steph knew that she wasn't being judged. There was a real chance.

"What do you have to lose?"

And Steph was going to tell her. She was going to confess her feelings. Get it out there. She could feel the words forming in the back of her throat. Feel them right there on the tip of her tongue, ready to be set free. But then a familiar squeak echoed through the lobby. A cart rolled into view. Steph's

259

mom sheathed her mop and wiped her forehead, then waved at her daughter.

"Who's your friend?" she asked as she came over to greet them.

"This is Mary." Steph quickly introduced them, thrown by her mother's appearance, by what she had almost admitted. "She moved here a few weeks ago."

"It's nice to meet you. Are you one of Steph's teammates?"

"Oh, no." Mary fielded the parental question like a pro. "I'm writing a story for the school paper. A profile on the team and its star player."

Mary nodded toward Steph, and Steph's mom lit up.

"Well, that's just great. I've been so proud of how much work she's put in these last couple of months. She's a star. The best daughter any parent could ask for. And you can quote me on that."

"Mom." Steph grimaced as her mother laughed at her own joke.

"I'm only kidding. Mary knows that."

But Steph could only roll her eyes. Usually she didn't mind her mom embarrassing her. But in front of Mary? Steph wanted to find a deep hole and bury herself in it.

"I should probably head out," Mary said, throwing her journal into her backpack. "Gotta get home before dark. But Steph, we should get together for some follow-up questions. Maybe this weekend?"

It took her a few seconds, but eventually Steph found her

voice, hoping it didn't shake with the nerves stirring up a thunder-storm in her belly.

"Sounds good to me."

And then Mary opened her arms and Steph, not knowing exactly what to make of it, came in for a hug. She held her breath as her chin nested on the top of Mary's shoulder, hoping the girl couldn't hear her pulse beating a furious pace against her neck. She counted the seconds as they passed. All the way up to eight before Mary let go and the two moved apart.

"I'll text you," Mary said, and then she was off, unsnapping her bike helmet from her backpack strap and positioning it on her head.

Steph watched her go, her heart still beating fast, her palms sweating. She watched without even realizing her mom was watching, too.

"She seems nice. And she's so cute with that short hair."

Steph blinked, turning to look at her mom, trying to figure out if there was some message hidden there in her words.

"She's been a good friend," Steph replied.

"I'm glad to hear it. Hopefully I'll get to see her around more."

Steph could only shrug, unsure of what exactly her mom meant.

"I'm going to start on my homework."

And Steph plopped down on one of the lobby benches. But as she pulled out her textbook, she knew she wouldn't be able to get anything done. Not with Mary on her mind.

CHAPTER 32
ELENA

"Are you almost ready?"

Elena didn't know what was taking so long.

"Give me a few more minutes," Grace replied, not bothering to look up as she consulted her little spell book. She dug into her bag and pulled out a piece of chalk and began carefully drawing a circle on the floor around the covered mirror.

"Do you have everything you need?" Elena glanced down at her phone and then back over to Grace.

"I think so."

Grace had finished with the protection circle and pulled several candles out of her bag, setting them in even intervals around the mirror. Then she got out a cheap lighter and lit them all, her hand clearly shaking as she went.

"Are you worried about your parents coming home?" Grace asked.

"They're in Des Moines," Elena said as she continued to stare at her phone. "They won't be home until tomorrow."

This didn't seem to comfort Grace, though. It was just the two of them, about to face a demon. But then who would they even call for backup? The fire department? They wouldn't be equipped to handle this either.

"We'll be fine," Elena said, more because she could tell that Grace needed to hear it than because she actually believed it herself. But it was her grandmother's legacy. She had to do this. Her plan had to work. There was no other way.

"You're right," Grace agreed, though she didn't sound so sure as she mumbled under her breath some more. "You're right. We can do this."

And then she got back to her preparations, pulling out a folded sheet of paper, going over her pronunciation guide again, following along with her finger, her mouth moving in unfamiliar motions as she silently practiced it to the end.

"I think I'm ready," Grace muttered.

"Good. Good." Elena waved her off, her eyes gleaming as a text message lit up her phone. Finally. "I'll be right back."

And before Grace could ask the question, Elena scurried out of the room, her heart beating quicker in her chest as she descended the stairs. Her plan was actually coming together.

"You made it," Elena exclaimed, slightly out of breath as she swung the front door open and found Mary there on the porch.

"You invited me," Mary replied with a shrug as she finished snapping her helmet around the handlebars of her bike, which she'd leaned up against the railing.

"Come in," Elena said, sticking her arm out like a lure. And Mary bit.

"Thanks for doing this on such short notice," Mary said. "I'm hoping to get the story done before you all head off to the district championships next week."

"It's not a problem," Elena replied, showing Mary where she could toss her coat. The interview request had actually saved Elena the trouble of coming up with a lie. If they were doing the ritual to trap the demon back in its mirror, they needed the demon to be there in the first place. "We can talk in my room."

And as Mary nodded, Elena led the way, heading up the stairs and into her grandmother's room, snapping the door shut quickly behind them.

"What's all this?" Mary jolted to a stop and Elena nearly ran into her. "Are you all having a sleepover? Trying to perform a séance?"

She had her notebook and pen out, and Elena could tell that she seemed more intrigued than frightened by the scene.

"Do you put hexes on your opponents or something? Is that your secret to winning?"

Elena ignored Mary's joking question and turned to Grace. "We're ready?"

But Mary's appearance had thrown Grace off.

"What's she doing here?" Grace stammered. "You promised it'd just be us."

"You want to save Calvin, don't you?" Elena pressed, her voice sharp, leaving no room for argument.

"Save who from what?" Mary butted in, but Elena didn't pay any attention to her. Instead, she floated across the room and took hold of the sheet covering the mirror. She yanked and it fell away, revealing the broken glass, more menacing than ever in the half-light, its shards wickedly sharp teeth ready to devour them all.

"Just read the spell," Elena commanded, speaking directly to Grace.

"What is all this?" Mary asked, sounding suddenly concerned.

"Don't act like you don't know." Elena turned on her. "I'm putting you back where you belong. You're not going to hurt anyone else."

"What are you talking about?"

Elena almost believed the girl's big doe eyes. The way her voice quivered with confusion. But she wasn't stupid. The demon was a trickster. Her grandmother had warned her of that. Elena wouldn't be fooled again.

"I'm getting out of here," Mary said, turning toward the door.

"You're not going anywhere."

And Elena launched herself across the room, pushing the girl up against the wall, using every inch of her small stature to pin Mary there.

"What the—" Mary started to shout, but Elena clapped her hand over the girl's mouth before she could finish.

"What are you doing to her?" Grace cried.

"Read the spell," Elena shouted.

"But—" Grace stuttered, clearly torn.

"Trust me. We have to put her back where she belongs."

Grace wavered for another second.

"She's the demon, Grace. Don't you see that? She showed up the day after I broke the mirror. Calvin drew her transformation in his notebook. I let her out and now we have to put her back in."

The explanation shot out of Elena's mouth. She didn't have time for Grace's doubt or indecision.

"Don't you want to save Calvin?"

And with that, reluctantly, Grace turned back to the mirror. She started the spell.

As she read the incantation out loud, Elena watched, digging her feet into the floorboards, using her legs to keep Mary's squirming body from escaping. The words were in a language that Elena couldn't begin to understand. But as they spilled out of Grace's mouth, something in the room shifted. Everything went still. The mirror seemed suddenly to take up every inch of space. It seemed to come alive. The glass pulsed with a fireside warmth, and the filigree detail running around its edge lit up, the letters of the forgotten language glowing as Grace read them, making a slow circle around the mirror's face.

A wind whipped through the room, tossing Elena's hair into her face. It flooded her ears like she was caught in a tornado. The windows rattled in their panes. The whole house seemed to shake. Elena thought they might be blown apart completely.

And then Grace finished the incantation. The last letters on the mirror glowed to life and completed the circle. The wind died down as suddenly as it'd started up and it was like they'd entered the eye of the storm, the mirror humming with light, glowing white hot.

Behind Elena, Mary bucked, kicking harder now, biting down on Elena's palm. Elena shouted but held on tight. This was it. She was going to put the demon back. She was going to lock it away and complete her grandmother's legacy. She worked her arms around Mary's shoulders and managed to spin her around, putting her closer to the mirror, the light pouring out of its face so bright it blinded them all.

"You're going back where you belong," Elena grimaced, her teeth gritted as she held Mary firm, pushing her forward one labored step at a time. "You're not going to hurt anyone ever again."

She was almost there. She gathered her strength for the final thrust. She closed her eyes and steeled her arms. She prepared herself to end this. But then Grace gasped. Elena's focus broke and she looked to the girl just ahead of her, saw confusion on Grace's face. Shock. Disbelief. Elena's gaze slid to the mirror and her heart stopped.

The white light glared for one more second, and then it dimmed, revealing a sheet of unbroken glass. And when it did, Elena felt her own scream come ripping up her throat.

It couldn't be. She'd followed her grandmother's note. She'd found the key in the mirror. She was putting the escaped demon back.

But then how could she explain the thing staring back at them, bloody palms pressed to the other side of the now unbroken glass? How could she make sense of those murderous eyes? Those teeth bared behind a wicked grin? How could she put the demon, Mary, back in the mirror if the demon was already there behind the glass?

"No. No. No." Elena heard herself saying out loud. This couldn't be happening. She couldn't have been wrong.

The mirror flashed bright, and this time it pulsed with a scorching heat, so hot that Elena had to turn away. When she looked back, her jaw dropped, but she was too afraid to let out a sound. The demon had pressed its face to the glass, its palms leaving smeared red handprints as it started to climb through the mirror. Grace leapt off the floor and scurried back to join Elena, the same fear in her eyes, in the what-have-we-done panic there.

What had they done?

Elena let go of Mary, the girl trembling from head to toe, frozen in disbelief and terror. Elena had roped her into this, too. She'd messed everything up.

Had the demon manipulated her this whole time? What had she been thinking? Flirting with random boys who turned out to be twelve-year-olds? Arguing with Henry? Fighting with Steph over the volleyball team? Convincing her that Mary was a demon? Why hadn't she seen through the tricks? How could she have been so wrong? How could she have lost?

A cackle rang through the room, creeping along the walls and floorboards like spiders with their eight scurrying legs. Elena's eyes grew big as she spotted the demon, floating there in front of them, completely free from the mirror. The tattered hem of its dress skimmed the ground. Its eyes glowed red, malicious and trained on Elena's face.

You don't look happy to see me.

The voice sounded so familiar, like Elena had been hearing it her entire life. It wasn't harsh or ugly, but somehow soothing. It swept her up. Drew her along. Lulled her to sleep.

But she couldn't let herself be fooled. This was the demon talking. This was evil. She had to remember that.

"You're not welcome here," Elena stuttered, squeezing the air through her lungs, barely getting the sound out. "No one invited you. Leave us alone."

It was your ancestor who first called on me.

Elena shook her head. Her grandmother had said their family had locked the demon away. They had guarded against her return. They hadn't summoned her.

I see you don't want to believe, little girl. But it's true. Your ancestor called on me because she wanted to take what her prettier sister had. Her looks. Her position. Her husband.

Elena shut her eyes and tried to block out the lies. They couldn't be true. Her family couldn't have brought this on themselves. She remembered the illustrations from the fairy tale book—the handmaiden working at the lady's feet, eventually replacing her, the bloody footprints leading to the mirror—and they suddenly all made sense.

Jealousy. Vanity. Fear. It makes humans so easy to control.

"No," Elena shouted, desperation flooding her voice. "What do you even want from me?"

The demon's lips split into a mirthful smile, another laugh spilling out of her, terrible in its glee. In the way it sounded certain that it'd already won.

Silly girl, I already have what I need from you. You brought me her.

And Elena gulped as the demon pointed a bony finger toward Mary, who had frozen on the spot.

Thank you for delivering my new vessel.

Elena's head whipped back and forth between the demon and the girl, not understanding.

"Vessel?"

My new host. I can only inhabit someone who has been given in sacrifice. And you've brought this girl right to me. Just as planned.

"You can't—" Elena stumbled over her words as she looked at Mary, who had backed up against the wall now, too shocked and too afraid to escape on her own. Paralyzed. Elena saw it all so clearly now. The way the demon had sprinkled in suspicion and used her rivalry against Steph. The way it'd planted the seeds of doubt, manipulated Elena to this point.

"I take it back," Elena shouted. "You can't have her."

It's too late for that. You've made your decision.

"No. You can't have her," Elena screamed, overwhelmed by it all. Desperate and afraid. Out of ideas. "Run, Mary!"

And this seemed to jolt the girl out of her daze. She pushed off the wall and made for the bedroom door. But before she could reach it, the demon appeared at her side, moving faster than Elena could see. It seized Mary's wrist and lifted her off the ground, dangling her there a foot above the floorboards, unfazed as the girl twisted and cried to get loose.

Be thankful it's this easy.

But Elena could only shake her head, tears leaking from her eyes. It wasn't easy. It was still a life given up.

Your ancestor would have sacrificed her own flesh and blood, but her daughter found out. She turned on her and trapped me in here. Would you not give me this girl? Someone you barely even know?

And Elena suddenly understood her family's history. Why they'd taken on this burden. Why she had to take it up now. Her great-great-great-whatever-grandmother had started it all, had summoned the demon out of jealousy and resentment, had been willing to sacrifice her own child to keep her youth and beauty.

But that daughter had stopped her. And their family had guarded over the mirror as a kind of penance ever since, a way to make amends for the evil their ancestor had brought into the world. Elena couldn't let that legacy down. She wouldn't be the failure in her family line.

"You can't have her," Elena growled, and she took a step toward the demon. She had to save Mary.

You think you can stop me?

And as Elena moved closer, she felt a sudden weight press down on her shoulders. Her knees buckled and she almost crashed to the floor. A sickly sweet perfume wafted under her nose and clawed its way down her throat, filling her lungs, making it harder and harder to breathe. She gasped for fresh oxygen. She struggled to stay upright as panic numbed her whole body. As Mary's screams filled her ears.

How was she supposed to stop a demon?

Elena's eyes fell to the side, looking to Grace, who was sitting there on the floor, her notes spread out all around her. She looked dazed and confused, like she'd bumped her head. Could she have a magic potion in her bag? Or a vanquishing spell hidden in her little book? Could Elena find a stake to drive through the demon's heart? Would that even work? Or was that only vampires?

Give up. It's hopeless. I already have what I need.

And with that, the demon turned its attention to Mary. It lifted its free hand to the girl's face, spreading its gnarled fingers over her cheeks. Mary shrieked as the demon dug its nails into her forehead, pressing her eyes open wide so that she couldn't turn away or hide.

"No," Elena whimpered, her energy spent, that weight still pressing down on her shoulders, her lungs still struggling to breathe.

She had to figure something out. She couldn't do nothing. But as Mary's whole body began to writhe in pain, as her cries grew more desperate and ragged, Elena realized she couldn't do this. She couldn't stop the demon. She couldn't save Mary. She was a failure. A loser.

With trembling fingers, she reached up to her neck and pulled on the thin silver chain. She fished her grandmother's locket out and stared at it, opening the clasp to look in at the picture of her ancestor, catching her reflection for a second in the miniature mirror there.

"I'm sorry," she whispered, and then she dipped her head in defeat, trying to block out Mary's screams. It was too late.

But just then, the bedroom door flew open. Two figures stood there for a moment, taking in the scene. Then they raced inside, Calvin's glasses glinting as he crouched to check on Grace and Steph's tall frame ramming full speed into the demon, knocking Mary loose from its grip.

"You can't take her!" Steph bellowed as she threw her arms out wide to cover Mary's body crumpled there on the floor. And Elena couldn't help but look at this girl with awe. She couldn't help but wonder when Steph had gotten so much braver than her.

CHAPTER 33
STEPH

Steph's arms quivered, the adrenaline drying up fast as her muscles screamed. What in the world had she walked in on?

Halloween had come a day early. And this thing in front of her—this grim reaper—wasn't a man in a costume and makeup. Those fangs weren't fake. That tangled hair wasn't a wig. Those bloodstains weren't ketchup mixed with corn syrup. It was all so very real. And it was trying to kill Mary. Her Mary.

Steph sneaked a glance behind her at the girl, who was lying in a whimpering heap on the floor, her wrist cradled close to her chest.

Step aside.

Steph's head snapped around at the demon's voice, and she felt her shoulder throb where she'd just run into it.

You can't keep me from my prize.

"It's going to be okay," Steph whispered, keeping Mary at her back. "I won't let it hurt you."

What do you think you can do?

Steph's pupils widened as the demon called her out.

You forget. I know your thoughts. Your heart. Your desires. I know you better than you know yourself. You're not strong enough to beat me.

A brittle cold seeped into the room, like Steph had plunged into an ice bath. Her arms grew heavier, and a weight pressed down on her chest. Her exhale sent a burst of frost into the air.

The demon had been in Steph's head for five years now. Ever since she'd stared into that stupid mirror. And in that time it'd seen her daydreams and darkest secrets. It knew her weaknesses and limitations. It knew *her.*

"I believe in you," Mary murmured, finding her voice even though she still couldn't get to her feet. It looked like she'd hurt her ankle, too, when the monster had dropped her.

As the words trickled into Steph's ears, a new hope ignited in her chest. Because the demon wasn't the only one who knew her. Hadn't she come out to Elena and Mary? Hadn't she finally come out to herself? If she could do that—what used to be the scariest thing imaginable—then what did she have to be afraid of now? She couldn't lose this. She couldn't lose Mary.

"You can't have her!" Steph shouted.

And before the demon could reply, she lunged forward and

grabbed the only weapon she could find—one of Elena's mom's decorative wooden scarecrows—off the dresser. She leveled it at the demon, knowing she must look stupid. But it was all she had. And a club was a club. The wooden figurine certainly felt heavy enough in her hand. She darted forward, swiping left and right. Keeping up the attack. Moving as fast as she could.

The demon danced away from each blow, avoiding them with ease. Its cruel laughter rang out through the room, taunting Steph, letting her know just how useless this all was. But Steph couldn't give up. She couldn't back down. She swung and swung and swung, her shoulder throbbing, the scarecrow growing heavier with each failed attack. Her breaths came shorter, and a pain opened up in her side until the demon suddenly reached out and caught her by the wrist, apparently tired of the game.

The demon's gaze met Steph's, holding it for a prolonged second. A fresh bloody tear slipped down its cheek. And then the demon lifted its other hand, a gust of wind pounding into Steph's chest, curling around her, crushing her in its grip. She shot backward, and the world exploded in bright, white pain as she slammed into the wall and slid to the floor, the demon turning its attention back on Mary.

"No." Steph grimaced, the air wheezing in and out of her lungs as she clawed her way forward, putting her body in front of Mary's again.

Didn't I warn you?

The demon moved closer.

You can't stop me.

"Doesn't mean I can't try." Steph scowled, her jaw aching from the effort.

No more games.

The demon reached forward, its bony fingers outstretched, ready to claw at Steph's face. Ready to end her in order to get to Mary. But as it closed the distance and Steph's eyes narrowed on the sharpened talons, a blur moved in the shadows. It launched itself across the room and slammed into the demon, dropping it to the ground in an impressive tackle.

"Get out of here!" Calvin yelled from the floor, his arms still wrapped around the demon's waist, keeping it pinned for as long as he could.

But the split second of surprise had already passed.

Foolish boy. I give you the gift of sight and this is how you repay me? You should have run when you had the chance.

The words slithered through the room as the demon flew out of Calvin's grasp and grabbed him by the arm. It held him there, his cheeks going white with fear.

Time for you to meet your fate.

The demon tossed Calvin over its shoulder, batting him away as easily as Steph would a volleyball. The boy sailed through the air, flying like a kite. Then he came crashing back to the ground, glass shattering and wood splintering as he collided with the antique mirror and rolled onto the floor.

Grace's scream ripped through the room then, but Steph couldn't stop to help. She had to keep her focus on the demon. The demon who'd turned around and started advancing on them again, a triumphant gleam in its eye, an arm ready to take what it thought belonged to it.

Steph could feel Mary's scared breath on her neck. She spotted Elena, and willed her to get up. To help. But the girl had gone dead in the eyes. Given up. She wasn't going to come to their rescue. And Steph couldn't fight this demon anymore. She could barely lift her arms. She didn't stand a chance.

She couldn't do anything. She couldn't save Mary. Her soulmate. She wasn't meant for that happy ending. She could only hold on to the girl. Hold on to her and finally let her know how she really felt.

"I like you," she whispered, realizing that her confession was already too late.

The demon leveled its gaze at Steph and then swatted her aside, knocking her away like a scarecrow doll. Then it reached for Mary, pressing its hand against her whimpering face. It squeezed the girl's eyes open and Mary's scream spilled into the room once more. A bloody tear fell from each of her eyes.

CHAPTER 34
GRACE

It was happening.

That was all Grace could think as the scream ripped out of her throat. As she watched Calvin fly across the room. As gravity caught him and slammed him back down in a terrible crash. As the antique mirror shattered into hundreds of pieces and Calvin's body flopped onto the floor, settling there amid the shrapnel.

It was happening. Fate had finally caught up with them. And there was nothing Grace could do about it.

Why had he followed her? Why had he tried to help? If he had just stayed out of it, then he would have been okay. He would have survived. He would have—

Grace's lungs constricted and her scream turned into a sob.

"Get up," she murmured, willing him to listen, praying that this wasn't the end he had drawn. "Please."

But he wasn't moving. She couldn't even tell if he was breathing.

Another sob hiccuped out of her, and she fought the urge to go to him. She'd seen the drawing. She knew the details. That he died with his head in her lap. She couldn't go to him. She couldn't fulfill that part of the prophecy. She couldn't make it come true.

But if this was it—she couldn't leave him there to die alone.

"Get up, get up, get up," she found herself murmuring. "Don't you dare die on me."

Tears welled up and blurred Grace's vision, turning Calvin into a dark splotch speckled with red polka dots. She let them pool, happy to lose the details. But then she had to blink. She tasted salt on her lips. Calvin's body snapped back into focus, the cuts flashing red on his face, his glasses thrown off and lost somewhere in the room, no sign of a breath lifting his chest. Still limp. Still gaunt. Gone.

A fresh scream filled the room, but Grace couldn't turn away from Calvin. She couldn't let him go. She couldn't accept that this was it.

And then his fingers twitched. They closed around an invisible pen, and Grace's heart leapt. He was still alive. And he needed her. She jumped to her feet and scurried across the room, doing her best to avoid the shards of broken glass littering the floor.

"I'm here, Calvin," she whispered, kneeling down and pulling his head into her lap. "Hold on for me. We're going to get through this. I'm not letting you go."

Calvin coughed, and Grace had never been so happy to hear him. To see him move. Even if he was in pain.

He groaned, but this time it sounded like he was trying to say something. So Grace leaned down close, pressing her ear to his mouth. His spit bubbled up and spattered against her cheek, but she still couldn't understand him.

"What?" Grace spoke urgently, feeling his time ticking away. "What are you trying to say? What do you need?"

"Help—them," Calvin managed to croak.

"But I—" Grace sputtered, lifting her head.

She'd only had eyes for Calvin. Had only thought of his life. She'd forgotten all about everyone else. But now she saw them. She saw the devastation—Elena frozen in fear, Steph beaten and sprawled out on the floor, Mary in the demon's grip, crying out in torture as the thing slowly poured its being into her body.

"I don't know how," Grace whimpered.

"You can do it."

And as Calvin uttered the words, his hand reached up and found Grace's, pressing a crumpled piece of paper into her palm.

"Save them," he gasped, and then fell silent, his head laid back on Grace's lap.

Tears slid down her cheeks. Her fingers balled into a fist, crunching the pronunciation guide she'd worked so hard on, the one that Calvin must have picked up off the floor. She glanced down at it, the symbols swimming in front of her.

He wanted her to save them. To lock the demon away for good. But how was she supposed to do that?

The incantation had failed. In fact, it'd done the opposite of what she'd thought. Grace had let the demon out. She'd given it the chance to find a new host. She couldn't figure out why it hadn't worked, though. She didn't know how to fix it. She'd translated it correctly. She was sure of that. She'd spent hours going over the pronunciation. And hadn't Elena's grandmother's note said that the key was in the mirror? The script was the only thing *in* the mirror. The only thing on it at all.

Grace lifted her fist and pounded it into the floor, shards of mirror clinking as she expelled her frustration. She'd done the work. She'd followed the clues. Nothing else made sense. It should have worked. It should have—

Grace punched the floor again, letting the paper fall from her hand.

The key was in the mirror. The key was in the mirror. The key was in the mirror.

She wanted to scream. She wanted to pulverize something. She swiped a piece of glass off the floor and pulled her arm back, ready to throw it at the demon because that was all she could think to do. But her own reflection twinkling in the glass stopped her. Her arm stilled and she stared at it. Locked eyes with herself, her pupils quivering. Thinking.

And then an idea struck her.

The key was *in* the mirror.

She grabbed the piece of glass and held it close to her paper guide, where she'd painstakingly written out the inscription and then filled in the pronunciation underneath. She stared at her writing and then at the shard of mirror. And right before her eyes, the incantation transformed, new words forming in the reflection. The right words—Grace was sure of it—hidden there *in* the mirror.

"I've got it," Grace breathed, not even believing it herself.

She stole a glance up at the demon. It still had Mary in its grasp. It still hadn't completed its transference. Grace still had time.

She held the mirror shard close to the page, her eyes whizzing over the words, trying to get some handle on it before she started. Luckily, it looked similar to the incantation she'd translated before. But she'd only have one shot at this. She couldn't screw it up.

She took one last glance down at Calvin, his eyes shut, his face contorted into a pained grimace, his chest barely rising and falling. It wasn't too late. She could still save him. She could save all of them. She swallowed and opened her mouth, the first words slipping from her lips in uncertain syllables.

But as Grace pushed on, something happened to her. The words somehow felt right in her mouth. Her voice grew louder and steadier. She was halfway through the incantation and she could feel the spell's power moving through her, bubbling up in her gut and spilling out of her mouth with each word.

It wafted into the room, growing in size, a beacon of light with Grace there in the middle. But Grace couldn't let herself get distracted. She couldn't get lost in the awe of it, in the power she was channeling into the room. She had to keep going.

Because the demon had noticed.

Its grip on Mary tightened, and the girl's screams intensified, filling the room, bouncing off the walls and shaking the windows in their panes.

Grace read on, pushing the words out as fast as she could. She had to finish. She had to lock the demon away.

It's over.

A triumphant cackle echoed through the room before Grace could finish. She'd run out of time. She wasn't going to save them.

And then, out of nowhere, Elena seemed to wake from her paralysis. The light from the spell that had poured into the room surrounded her, pushing her forward. She launched herself off the ground and leapt across the room, wrapping her hands around the demon's wrists, yanking them away from Mary and holding them steady. A fire reflected in her eyes that could have burned up the whole room.

"Finish the spell," Elena shouted over the demon's roar, her hair whipping in the breeze, the light reflecting off its golden strands, her grandmother's locket dangling from her neck.

And hope welled in Grace's chest. She focused her whole attention on the reversed spell, speaking as loudly and clearly as she could, pronouncing every word like her life depended on it.

She made it to the last line.

Only four words left now.

Then two syllables.

As Grace reached the end of the incantation, her teeth biting off the last letters, she threw her head back to see. Across the room, the demon screamed, writhing with fury to get out of Elena's grasp. But Elena refused to let go. Somehow she'd held on.

The light that had poured into the room when Grace had started reading the spell flickered. It flashed like lightning, popping and crackling, dancing around Elena and the demon. The air hummed with energy, loud and large, ready to blow. And then a final bolt cracked through the room, heading straight for Elena, striking her directly in the chest.

But it hadn't hit her in the chest. It'd connected with her locket, the silver metal glowing, smoking as its light reflected off the walls and the hundreds of pieces of shattered glass littering the floor, dazzling like a disco ball. But it didn't stop there. The light grew. It became a blinding flash that blanketed the room in white. And then it imploded.

A boom echoed through the room, a tornado pulling everything to its center. Grace braced herself to keep from flying away, holding on to Calvin as the wind whipped all around them. A howl cut through the noise and Grace saw the demon lifted off its feet, its mouth frozen in a furious snarl. The light flashed one last time and then disappeared, throwing the room into darkness. Leaving behind an eerie stillness.

Grace stared into the pitch black, her breath heaving in her chest, her mouth dry, her throat aching from shouting her way through the incantation. She strained to see if the spell had worked. To see if the demon had vanished.

And slowly, the daze from the blinding light faded. Her night vision kicked in and she could see again. Calvin's head in her lap. Steph and Mary crumpled on the floor. And Elena standing all by herself in the center of the room, her grandmother's locket pulsing against her neck, keeping time with her heartbeat.

And the demon—there was no sign of it. It was gone.

Grace squinted, not believing her eyes. Not believing that it actually could have worked.

"We did it," she murmured.

Tears filled her eyes. Happy, relieved ones, for once. And she turned her gaze down to Calvin to celebrate.

"It's gone."

But the joy quickly died in her throat.

"Calvin?"

She tapped his cheeks. She shook his shoulders, trying to wake him.

He couldn't—

She'd locked the demon away.

The curse was over.

She'd saved him.

"Calvin?"

CHAPTER 35
CALVIN

The wind whipped all around him as Calvin fell, snatching away every breath he tried to take. He didn't have any clue where he was or how he'd gotten there. Only that his body was trapped in the whirlwind of an unknown tornado, pitching and plummeting in the pitch black.

He was falling. Or was he flying?

His eyelids fluttered open and he could see stars, the pinpricks of light so far away, winking in the distance. They were so pretty. So dazzling. Did they want to tell him something?

He squinted and tried to read a code in their pulsing. He perked up his ears and strained to hear anything over the roaring wind. But nothing came through. It was only nonsense. Impossible to understand. And he was getting tired, his head growing heavy, his eyes drooping.

It didn't matter. He could figure it out later. Right now he just wanted to lie back and let the winds carry him away. Let them sweep over him, pull him under their churning currents. He couldn't remember the last time he'd felt so relieved. So unworried. It was like a knife's edge had been removed from his neck, and he could relax for the first time in years.

He could sleep.

His head tipped back and his eyes closed. The wind wrapped him in its arms, held him tight as it tugged him down into its spiral. Pulling him deeper into the darkness, the stars growing farther away with each passing second.

He felt at peace. Finally. Ready to slip away.

But then something called out to him, a whisper carrying underneath the wind. His head twitched to the side. Who was calling to him? What were they trying to say?

Calvin . . .

It was a voice so familiar, but he couldn't place it.

Calvin . . . look at me.

His eyes opened, the stars pulsing brighter, sending spears of light down through the darkness.

A face floated there in front of him, reflected in the starlight.

Calvin . . . come back to me.

The whisper found him again. And this time, he thought he knew it. It belonged to a girl. *The* girl.

Calvin . . . don't leave me alone.

And he couldn't. He couldn't move on without her.

He turned in the air, fighting against the wind. He forced himself free of its grasp and swam through the tornado, kicking his legs and stroking his arms. He pushed through the gale. He reached for the stars. And he finally broke through, gasping for air, leaving the darkness behind as he woke up.

Water dripped against his cheeks as he opened his eyes and saw her—Grace—sobbing over him, her face hovering inches above his. He saw the moment she realized he'd woken up. The instant she knew he wasn't dead.

"You made it," she breathed, apparently too worn out to shout.

"I'd never abandon you," Calvin whispered, and before he knew it, Grace had pressed her lips to his, kissing him, bringing him back to life all over again.

"Is it gone?" Calvin asked, pulling away from Grace slowly, his head still buzzing from his near-death experience. Or maybe that was just the kiss. "Did the spell work?"

"See for yourself."

And Grace helped Calvin sit up straight, his head still throbbing from his collision with the mirror.

Across the room, Steph had crawled over to check on Mary, who looked shaken up but okay. Then above them Elena stood all by herself, the locket open in her hand as she studied the miniature portrait and mirror inside. Calvin watched as she snapped it shut and tucked it underneath her shirt, her hand hovering over it, keeping it safe.

He didn't see the demon anywhere. But that didn't mean—

He held his hand out in front of him and focused on his fingers. But they didn't tremble. They didn't even twitch. He strained to hear the voice in the back of his head sending him premonitions of doom. But again, there was nothing. No flashes of the future. No deadly omens. Just quiet. Peace. And Grace sitting beside him.

"It's really gone," Calvin murmured as he squeezed Grace's hand in his. "You did it. You broke the curse. You saved me."

EPILOGUE
ELENA

A whistle blew, long and shrill, and a quiet hum fell over the stands, the crowd leaning forward, on the edge of their seats for the upcoming match point. On the court, Elena bent low near the net, her entire focus trained on the opposing server, watching as the girl tossed the ball up into the air and sent it flying.

She turned as the ball crossed the net, following its downward trajectory with her eyes. Julia was there underneath it, bracing herself for the pass. And then it'd be Elena's turn to take over, to set the ball for the championship kill. But instead of bumping right to where Elena stood in the center of the court, the ball twisted up Julia's forearms, shooting off to the side. Elena's legs tensed and she sprinted after it, calling for her teammates to get out of the way. She needed to get under it. To set it perfectly. To get their team the win.

She slid forward at the last second, her knee pads scraping the floor as she wriggled underneath the ball, both hands spread into a setter's basket. The leather brushed against her fingertips and she popped it right back out, throwing it across the court, shouting out "FOUR" at the top of her lungs, trusting that Steph would be there.

And sure enough, Steph's tall figure launched into the air, her arm pulled back, moving forward and around in a smooth motion. She struck the ball cleanly and it zoomed across the net, flying into the back corner of the court.

Whistles blew again, and the crowd started cheering. But it was nothing compared to the screams of Elena's teammates, to the players rushing from the bench, dogpiling on top of her as they celebrated their win. Their championship.

In all the whipping ponytails and long limbs clapping her on the back, Elena managed to get to her feet. She glanced across the court and saw that Steph had gotten the same treatment, the other half of the team celebrating with her. She watched her, the girl's face lit up with joy, the cuts and bruises healing nicely already. Elena couldn't understand how she had ever hated her. She couldn't think of why she'd thought she could have done it all on her own.

And then their eyes met. Held.

"You did it," Elena mouthed, smiling big, afraid that the girl might not believe her.

"*We* did it," Steph replied, and Elena knew that things were going to be okay between them. That Steph might forgive her one day.

Elena watched as Steph broke away from the pack of girls and jogged across the court, her arms uplifted as she neared the bleachers where Mary was waiting for her.

Steph launched herself into the girl's embrace and the two did a little victory dance. Other than the brace Mary had on her wrist, Elena wouldn't have known that they'd barely survived a run-in with a demon only a week before.

The two pulled apart as Steph's mom and brother walked up behind them. At first, Elena worried what they might say, but Steph's mom only reached around and hugged both the girls, her younger brother racing around them, jumping up and down in celebration. Elena couldn't help but notice as Steph slipped her hand into Mary's, nuzzling her curly head onto the girl's shoulder, her smile brighter and happier than Elena had ever seen it.

Freer.

Blinking, Elena looked away, not wanting to interrupt the moment or make it awkward for Steph. Her gaze traveled over the stands, and she spotted a different pair. Grace and Calvin. Sitting close together, Grace chatting away as Calvin worked over his notebook.

For a second, Elena's heart pounded, afraid of what Calvin might have seen, a prophecy coming to life on the paper. But then he picked up his head, a laugh brightening his face as

Grace finished her story. He still looked a little beat up from his run-in with the mirror, but he'd outlived his fate. And Elena had to remind herself that his visions were gone. The demon couldn't get to them. The curse had been broken.

A motion caught Elena's attention. She cringed, but then saw it was only Grace waving. She must have noticed something in Elena's look, because she tapped Calvin on the shoulder and took the notebook out of his hands. She held it up, and Elena could just barely make out the picture, what she realized was the night's winning shot, a girl lifted herself off the ground to spike the ball over the net and then another girl crouched low on the ground, watching her set soar into the right place.

Elena returned the gesture with her own thumbs-up. With the hope that she and Grace could be friends again. Best friends, like they'd been years ago. Grace had saved them. She'd figured out the spell. And for that, Elena would always owe her. Would always be appreciative.

"Congratulations."

Elena turned, surprised to see Henry there beside her, the cast still covering his whole right arm. She hadn't even realized he'd been there in the stands to watch.

"You were great out there," Henry went on.

"Thanks," she replied, not quite knowing what to say to him.

"You reminded me of the old Elena."

And to this, Elena could only blush. Could only nod as

Henry kept walking, glancing back over his shoulder at her once, and then twice. Could only wonder if maybe they still had that shot at soulmate-dom after all.

Her hand moved up to her chest and pressed down, feeling the locket under her jersey, the metal warm beneath her fingertips, pulsing steadily, giving off its own heartbeat. She shut her eyes and listened. She could just make out the whisper of a voice. Something trying to worm its way into her ear. Trying to trick her. But she knew better now. Knew how to recognize and ignore it.

She shook her head and the whispers disappeared.

Her hand stayed at her chest, though, gripping the locket tight. It was her burden to carry now. Her turn to take up her family's legacy. She wouldn't let her grandmother down. And if the demon ever did get too much for her to handle, she knew where she could find backup. Knew who she could rely on.

She wasn't alone in this fight. Not anymore.

ACKNOWLEDGMENTS

Creating a book takes more than just the author. There are a number of people working behind the scenes who turn the words in my head into the thing sitting there on your shelf. I am grateful to every single one of them.

First off, I'd like to thank everyone at Scholastic for giving me the opportunity to bring Bloody Mary to life. Samantha Palazzi, my incredible editor. David Levithan who's been a friend and inspiration. Also a big thank you to all of the people who have worked on this book behind-the-scenes. To the cover artist, Mirekis (Mirosław Iskra), and the designer, Yaffa Jaskoll. To the production editor, Janell Harris, the copy editor, Jessica White, and the proofreaders, Peter Kranitz, Susan Hom, and Cindy Durand. To the Fairs and Clubs managers Jana Haussman and Kristin Standley. To the publicist, Alex Kelleher-Nagorski. And a particular shout-out to the sales team. I appreciate all of the hard work you've done to get my book out into the world and onto bookshelves everywhere.

I'd also like to thank my family—my mom and dad and brother. I wouldn't be a writer without them. And thanks to my critique partner, Robby Weber, for his insight, notes, and friendship. He was the first to read each chapter, and his enthusiasm helped propel me through to the end. Also, a big thank you to my agent, Brent Taylor, and to everyone at Triada US.

I started drafting this book at the beginning of the COVID-19 pandemic, and it was the escape I needed from everything happening around the world. I'm thankful for my partner, Kyle, and my three best furry/feathered friends— Orisa, Mochi, and Rio—who kept me entertained and sane throughout, while also giving me the space I needed to write.

And to my readers, thank you for all of your support.

7/22-O